Daniel said softly, 'A kiss, for charity, wasn't that the deal?'

She shook her head, her throat tight, and she would have backed away, except that the thought of James shinning up the spire seemed to have paralysed her limbs. Or perhaps it was Daniel himself.

He watched her, his eyes narrowed, glittering beneath a veil of thick black lashes. Then his mouth brushed hers, and a tremor of something vibrant and shocking rippled over her lips. She wrenched herself away from him.

Daniel studied her, one dark brow lifting. 'What's wrong, Laura?' he queried coolly. 'I don't recall you being so reticent before.'

Laura gasped. 'You knew. . .you *knew*. . .I thought——'

His firm mouth indented in a way that made her nerves leap. 'Did you really believe this outfit you're wearing could throw me off track?' He shook his head. 'How could I ever forget you, Laura?' he gritted harshly. 'Don't you know you're imprinted on my mind like a laser burn?'

For Terry, Mark and Kerry

WILD HEART

BY

JOANNA NEIL

MILLS & BOON LIMITED
ETON HOUSE   18–24 PARADISE ROAD
RICHMOND   SURREY   TW9 1SR

First published in Great Britain 1990 by Mills & Boon Limited

© Joanna Neil 1990

Australian copyright 1990 Philippine copyright 1991 This edition 1991

ISBN 0 263 76929 1

Set in 11 on 13 pt Linotron Times 05-9104-42211 Typeset in Great Britain by Centracet, Cambridge Made and printed in Great Britain

CHAPTER ONE

THIS was the very last time she would allow herself to be drawn into one of James's reckless schemes, Laura vowed fretfully, pacing the gravelled sweep of the wide avenue. One of these days, he was going to go too far, and land himself in a lot of trouble. . .that was, if he ever managed to get down safely from that tower, of course.

Her glance shot hurriedly to the old university building, standing tall and solid against the grey skyline. She shivered, and rubbed her hands over her bare arms, feeling chilled in the cool evening air. The long skirt of her dress, with its full, flouncing lace petticoats, hampered her movements, and she swished it up impatiently with her fingers.

It was a foolhardy venture, just typical of the wild, carefree behaviour that she had come to expect of James. Laura cast another anxious look in the direction of the bell-tower. She could just make out his figure in the darkness, beginning the precarious ascent of the wall. It was far too dangerous. If only she could have put him off this wretched stunt—but there had been no chance, he had been determined on it, whatever she had said.

'Stop worrying, will you, Laura?' he'd insisted, his hazel eyes bright with tolerant amusement. 'You don't belong to the university, so you're not going to get into any trouble.'

'That isn't the point,' she had argued. 'It isn't safe, for one thing——'

'I've been on climbing expeditions before, and I've all the tackle I need, so there's no need to get yourself into a state. Just think of all the money we'll collect for charity—we can give odds on how long the trousers will stay up on the belltower before the Dean gets wind of it—or how long it takes to get them down again—we could even——'

'Don't—don't get carried away,' Laura had put in, taking a deep breath. 'Just think about how mad the Dean is going to be when he finds out— not to mention your mother and. . .' She'd bitten her lip in agitation. She had been going to add 'and Daniel', but her throat had closed up at the thoughts that James's half-brother inspired in her; better that Daniel Warwick remained in the dark recesses of her mind—at least it was less painful that way.

'They aren't going to find out who's responsible, are they?' James had cast her objections aside airily. 'I doubt anyone will be around to see what's going on, they'll most probably all be in the pubs, celebrating after the pageant. And anyway, that's where you come in—you can distract anybody who does happen to come along.' He'd grinned at her. 'In that get-up, no one will be looking anywhere but at you.'

She bared her teeth at him. She was hardly anything but conspicuous in her eighteenth-century costume, and, much as he might laugh, she didn't find the situation funny in the least. If she had any sense at all, she'd be back at the flat, adding the finishing touches to the painting she had been restoring, not to mention the cleaning she had to do. Maggie was due back from her assignment in the States tomorrow, and she ought at least to whip a duster round the place.

'Lighten up, Laura,' James had chided. 'I mean to end my last year at university with a bang.'

Laura shuddered now, thinking back on that conversation. She wished he had not phrased it quite that way.

She tugged at her tightly laced bodice and tried to adjust the folds of silk which persisted in slipping from her shoulders. So far, no one had ventured this way, but it was too much to hope for that her luck could last.

Just lately, things had had a nasty habit of going wrong. Her father's last, and fatal, heart attack had been a terrible shock that had knocked her sideways for some time.

She shook her bright auburn curls so that the

mob-cap she wore quivered precariously. She wouldn't let herself become morose. Things were looking up, after all. Sharing the flat with Maggie was fun, and there was her freelance work to keep her busy, commissions to restore art work that sometimes led to her travelling around, seeing a bit more of the world than she had done hitherto. It was what she had trained for, after all.

A slight, muffled sound disturbed the air, and her thoughts came back to her present precarious situation with a jolt. She peered into the darkness. Someone was coming from the lodge. Her breath caught in her chest. Another figure appeared in the glow from the doorway, and the two people, two men, seemed to be talking quietly. She watched, tensing as a door closed, and the man who had come out of the house started to walk along the drive towards the tree-lined avenue.

He was halfway along the avenue when she heard pebbles rattle over the ground in the distance, and she felt her throat close in dismay. James must have disturbed something.

The man shot a glance over his shoulder, and Laura hurried forward, anxious to distract his attention from the tower. He turned back as she approached, stopping suddenly, as if she had startled him, and Laura saw his face properly for the first time, and was frozen into immobility. Shocked disbelief drained the colour from her face. James's half-brother, here, now? She almost groaned aloud. It couldn't be. Surely it wasn't possible? Daniel Warwick was overseas; how was it that he could show up here, tonight of all nights, as if her dark thoughts had served to conjure him up out of nowhere?

She moved back into the shadows thrown out by the overhanging branches of the horse-chestnuts that lined the drive, clinging to the faint hope that he might be in a hurry and pass her by.

He didn't. He stared at her, moonlight throwing the hard planes and angles of his features into harsh focus. His grey eyes narrowed, shifting over her with cool, unhurried precision, and she sent up a silent prayer that he might not know her under the cover of night.

'It must be later than I realised,' he said at last, and his voice was deep and gritty, tingling along her nerve-endings just as it had always done. 'My imagination is beginning to play tricks on me. Or can it be true that the campus is haunted, after all?'

She felt light-headed all at once, insubstantial, as if the earth was shifting beneath her feet. She had seen him once, briefly, in the four years since he had left England to concentrate on his business concerns abroad; four years, and she could still feel all the hurt and disillusion as if it had been yesterday. There were times when he'd paid fleeting visits home, but she had taken care to avoid him. She had not been ready for a confrontation.

It was only at her father's funeral that she had been taken unawares, when his unexpected appearance had the effect of fuelling the smouldering resentment that had gathered inside her. She had tried to ignore him, but that was never an easy thing to do. There was no denying that he had a forceful presence, an aura of power that made him stand out in a crowd. His authority was tangible, underlined in the firm, clean-cut angle of his jaw, in the alert, shrewd intelligence of those dark eyes.

He moved towards her now, and Laura took an uncertain step backwards, hitching up the hem of her long gown, her billowing skirts rustling as she moved.

How could this be happening to her? Why had she let James get her into this situation? She blinked up at Daniel, her heartbeat quickening under his penetrating scrutiny.

'Now why are you here, I wonder? What would bring such a beautiful apparition to this place?' His dark brows lifted questioningly and Laura lowered her lashes, worrying at her lip with small white teeth. Was it possible that he did not recognise her? Surely he would have acknowledged her differently if he had known who she was?

The darkness was a shroud, of course, and she was well aware that she looked nothing like her usual self. Apart from the fancy-dress costume, which must have thrown him, she was wearing her hair loose instead of in the neatly pinned style she generally opted for. The realisation helped restore her shattered composure a little.

'Aren't you going to explain?' he prompted, his cool grey stare flicking over her. 'What is it that you want? Have you come to steal an unwary heart?'

Her green eyes widened. Had she imagined the undercurrent of cynicism that laced his words? 'Do you have a heart to give?' she countered.

His mouth twisted, and then he startled her, moving suddenly to circle her wrist with his strong fingers, drawing her towards him. 'Find the answer for yourself,' he gritted softly, his gaze streaking the tumbled mass of red-gold hair that fell across her face. 'Touch me. Feel the pulse of my blood and tell me if I have, or not.'

She tried to pull back, but there was no way she could fight off the iron band that held her fast. Her fingertips encountered the warmth of his skin through the thin covering of his shirt, and the contact had an electric, scorching quality to it that took her breath away. She jerked her hand as if she had been burned and this time he let her go, mockery glinting in his dark eyes. She wanted desperately to escape, to break free from the magnetic flux that surged between them. He was her enemy. She had to remember that.

But how could she get away? She darted a quick

look towards the tower, but James was still clearly outlined there; he had not gained his objective. If Daniel should see him. . . She did not like to think what the consequences would be. She didn't like to think of the trouble which could ensue if Daniel found out about his brother's latest escapade.

'Something appears to be troubling you,' he murmured, his voice tinged with irony. 'You're very tense.'

Laura shivered under his probing glance. When she didn't answer, he went on, 'You still haven't told me why you are out here.' His dark head shifted, and for a frantic moment she thought he was about to turn and look back at the tower.

She said, hurriedly, 'I was on my way home. I took part in the pageant—did you see it? We were collecting for charity—for a number of charities.' The words tumbled from her lips, then she came to a stumbling halt, looking at him, a frown marring her brow.

'I saw some of it. I was on my way to keep an appointment.' He paused, allowing his glance to stray over her features and run smoothly over her slender curves, outlined in the tight-waisted dress. Heat filled her cheeks as his gaze wandered with cool insolence over the creamy expanse left bare by the scalloped bodice. She made a restless movement, and he said in a lazy drawl, 'You must have made a tidy sum of money. I couldn't help but notice the way that some of the girls were collecting donations, though unfortunately I didn't have time to sample the wares myself.'

Laura stared at him blankly, not understanding, and his dark gaze slid to the soft, full curve of her mouth. When the meaning of his words sank in, she felt the swift flood of colour sweep her cheeks. He thought she had been selling kisses, but it had been the students doing that; she had been content to shake her collecting tin at passers-by.

'Is it a fixed price,' he murmured, 'or does it increase according to the level of involvement?'

She eyed him coldly, her body stiffening. 'I wouldn't know,' she said. 'That wasn't my——'

More pebbles skittered in the distance, and she broke off, shooting a worried look in James's direction. He was all right, thank heaven. He had almost reached the top. Relief washed over her for an instant, before she dragged her scattered wits together and gave her attention to Daniel Warwick once more. He was watching her closely, his face hard-boned, shuttered. Shifting position, he slanted his glance over the grey-shrouded university building, and she said tautly, 'What a pity you only managed to see a little of the pageant.'

He turned back to her. 'It is, isn't it? But perhaps I could make up for something that I missed.' She tensed at the dark, brooding quality of his expression, a swift prickle of apprehension running along her spine, up to the nape of her neck. She was uncomfortably aware of his long, lean height, of the breadth of his shoulders beneath his open jacket, of the short space that separated them.

His long fingers played over her wrist, and she looked up at him in alarm. He said softly, 'A kiss, for charity, wasn't that the deal?'

She shook her head, her throat tight, and she would have backed away, except that the thought of James shinning up the spire seemed to have paralysed her limbs. Or perhaps it was Daniel himself.

He watched her, his eyes narrowed, glittering beneath a veil of thick black lashes.

He moved closer, his head tilting towards her, and she heard distant, muted sounds, metal clinking on stone.

Then his mouth brushed hers, and a tremor of something vibrant and shocking rippled over her lips. She wrenched herself away from him.

Daniel studied her, one dark brow lifting. 'What's wrong, Laura?' he queried coolly. 'I don't recall you being so reticent before. But perhaps that was because you were on home ground, back at the cottage.'

Laura gasped. 'You knew. . .you *knew*. . . I thought——'

His firm mouth indented in a way that made her nerves leap. 'Did you really believe this outfit you're wearing could throw me off track?' He shook his head. 'How could I ever forget you, Laura?' he gritted harshly. 'Don't you know you're imprinted on my mind like a laser burn?' He dragged her towards him, and her stunned senses registered the hard impact of his body, and the searing, sensual glide of his hand as it stroked the length of her spine.

A shiver of alarm ran through her, making a pulse quiver and begin to hammer violently in her throat.

'Take your hands off me,' she said through her teeth, pushing ineffectually at the hard wall of his chest with her trembling fingers.

He ignored her, reaching up to pluck the mob-cap from her tawny curls. 'I like your hair like this,' he muttered, the heat of his glance shimmering over her.

She tried to retrieve the scrap of cotton and lace. 'What do you think you're doing? Let me go, damn you!' she flared, her voice shaking with the panic that surged in her chest.

His fingers threaded through the silk of her hair, curving around her nape. 'Of course—when you've said hello nicely.'

He bent his dark head towards her, and she said in a choked, angry voice, 'I'd sooner shake hands with a wolf than have anything to do with you.' She tried to twist out of his grasp, but there was too much controlled strength, too much unleashed power in his taut, lean frame for her struggles to be of any use. 'I wish I'd never met you,' she bit out.

'It's too late for that,' he drawled. 'Four years too late.' The warmth generated by his hand at her waist and hip dominated her consciousness, invading her body with a hot, sweeping sensation. Unwillingly her gaze transferred to the firm line of his mouth, tracing its contours with a nervous compulsion.

'No,' she whispered hoarsely, turning her head away and making a desperate effort to get away from him. His hold on her did not slacken; instead, she felt herself being drawn by the warm pressure of his palm, slowly, inexorably, ever closer to him. She was folded into the solid, muscled wall of his body, so that her breasts were crushed softly against his chest, and she could feel the steady thud of his heartbeat next to her own.

He tilted her face towards him and then his mouth came down on hers, stifling the small, choked sound of protest that had half formed in her throat.

She tried to keep her mind separate from what was happening to her, willing herself to remain passive under the siege of his lips. Hadn't he been responsible for all the torment of the last few years, for the stress that her father had undergone? Hadn't she every reason to mistrust him? She could not let the urgent, demanding pressure of his kiss pervade her senses.

He was dangerous to her, lethal—so why was it that he could make her blood race along her veins like wildfire, filling every crevice of her being with heated sensation? How was it possible that she could melt into the seductive embrace of his lips and hands?

He dragged his mouth from hers, at last, and she stared at him, dazed with shock. Her limbs were weak; if he had not been supporting her, she might have fallen.

He studied her, and she knew her eyes must reflect her bewilderment, but, try as she might, she could not seem to free herself from the heavy languor that his kisses had induced.

He touched the silk tendrils of her hair that had strayed across her cheek, then allowed his fingers to trail, whisper-light, over her skin to stroke the ripe curve of her mouth.

'You're beautiful,' he muttered. 'A siren to lure men to their doom.' A half-smile played lazily around his mouth, but it was not a smile that held any warmth. His fingers shifted, to discover the smooth nakedness of her shoulder, then feathered down over the sweeping slope of her breasts. A soft gasp of shock escaped her lips.

'Don't do that,' she protested, shame and resentment combining to add fiery heat to her cheeks. 'Keep your hands to yourself.'

His dark eyes mocked her. He slid the silky folds of material back up over her bare shoulders, making her skin tingle where his fingers touched, and she pulled away from him, angry with him, angry with herself for reacting to him as she had done.

'There was a time when you were much more encouraging towards me,' he jibed, his lips curling. 'But then, it was all an act, wasn't it, Laura? You knew what you wanted, and you weren't about to let anything get in your way.'

'It wasn't like that,' she denied huskily.

'Wasn't it?' A dark brow edged upwards. 'You'd have to work hard to convince me of that. Why don't you try?' he invited silkily. 'You almost persuaded me once before, but I managed to resist the temptation. Maybe you could do better this time.'

His taunts cut into her like a whiplash, and she hated him for it. 'You flatter yourself,' she returned scornfully. 'If our paths hadn't crossed I'd have forgotten your existence. I've seen so little of you these last few years I'd put you right out of my mind.'

He stared at her, his eyes hooded. 'Had you? I'm almost led to believe that you might have been avoiding me deliberately.'

She quirked a brow upwards. 'I'm afraid I don't follow.'

'Don't you? The fact that I bought your property wouldn't have prompted any desire for communication, I suppose—even if it was only to gloat over the high price you managed to exact?'

Laura ignored the barb, making herself shrug lightly. 'Hardly. You were abroad. If I did have any problems your agent and I managed to sort them out quite adequately between us.'

'Perhaps. But I have been back from time to time, and there were occasions when I might have appreciated dealing with you myself.' He eyed her consideringly. 'You were never available, though, were you, Laura? There was always some urgent reason why you just happened to be away when I managed to schedule a meeting.' He paused. 'I wonder why, if you were as indifferent to me as you'd have me believe.'

She frowned. 'It doesn't signify anything,' she answered coolly. 'I've been busy—just as you have been, from all accounts, extending your empire, adding to your art collection here and there.' Her mouth shaped a grimace. 'But you're never satisfied, are you? There is always something more that you must have.'

'You could well be right,' he drawled. 'Maybe we should talk about it?' His glance moved over her, appraising her from head to toe with a slow deliberation that made her skin burn.

'I don't have time to play games,' she said coldly. 'And neither, I imagine, do you. Presumably you're back in Dorset for a reason?'

His gaze hardened, then he said drily, 'I'm over here to pay James a visit, since you ask. And, of course, there are one or two matters that need my attention—the cottage shop, for instance.'

'Oh yes,' Laura acknowledged tightly. 'The shop was always high on your list of priorities, wasn't it? You must have found it galling to have to wait such a long time to get your hands on it.' She took a breath to steady the shake in her voice. 'But now that's all finished, isn't it? You got what you wanted in the end. At least my father wasn't around to see it happen.'

That was her main consolation—that and the fact that Daniel had been forced to put in the highest bid for the property she had inherited on Calum's death. 'What will you do now? Will you raze it to the ground and build a concrete and glass store in its place?'

He ignored her outburst. 'I was sorry to hear about your father,' he said quietly.

'Were you?' She threw him a cold glance. 'It was the stress that did it, finally, you know. The worry of trying to keep his head above water and cling on to what he had. But the struggle proved just too much for him in the end. His heart gave out.' Bitterness edged her voice.

He said, 'He could have made things easier for himself. He chose otherwise.' Daniel's mouth firmed. 'I had a flight booked immediately after the funeral, otherwise you and I might have talked. It was long overdue.' He assessed her thoughtfully. 'What of you? How are you coping?'

Laura stiffened. 'Please don't insult me by feigning an interest,' she said icily, starting to turn away along the drive. She did not want to be with him like this, to have to speak to him any longer, raking over dead leaves. It was too painful—her nerves were too raw.

Surely James must be through by now? She didn't want to have him come face to face with Daniel; he'd been in enough trouble over his escapades just lately, and she doubted that his climbing expedition would sit favourably with his autocratic brother.

'Has your companion finished the deed, then?' Daniel queried softly, stopping her in her tracks.

She swung round, her gaze transfixed. When she continued to stare at him in complete and utter shock, he said, 'Of course I knew. Did you think you could fool me? Though I confess, it comes as a surprise to find you helping someone out.' His voice was cold with derision. 'I'm just wondering what must be in it for you.'

Laura clenched her teeth. 'I can't think why I'm listening to this—you obviously have a warped mind. I almost feel sorry for you.'

'I take it that he must be wealthy? Is that the answer, Laura? Have you found someone else to solve your problems for you?'

She felt a surge of anger stab inside her. Who was he to attempt to judge her? She thought of James, and the substantial inheritance that would one day be his, and a cool little smile crossed her lips.

'As it happens,' she said, keeping her tone even, 'he does have the promise of extreme wealth. Does that satisfy your curiosity?' She did not wait for an answer. 'Now, if you'll excuse me, I really do have to go.'

This time, he did not try to stop her. Moonlight threw his features into harsh relief, highlighting the strong bones, the hard, uncompromising line of his mouth. Laura brushed past him, her body stiff and cold. She wanted to put as much distance between herself and Daniel Warwick as was humanly possible. He was insufferable.

It was just as well that he spent the greater part of his time abroad. She need never run into him again.

The two half-brothers were not very much alike, Laura reflected, as James walked towards her a few minutes later. Even though they had shared the same father.

James had dark brown hair, usually worn a little too long, so that it vied with his collar. His features were pleasantly put together, hazel eyes that often appeared brooding, a gentle-looking mouth that could be sullen, but more often was curved in easy laughter. No, he was not at all like his brother.

'I did it, you see, Laura,' he said cheerfully, as

he handed her into the passenger seat of his car. 'I told you it would be a piece of cake.'

'So you did,' she muttered. His car was a low, flashy sports model, because James liked speed; rather too much, Laura thought at times. 'Maybe you should thank heaven you're still in one piece,' she remarked grimly.

He shot her a sideways glance. 'What's wrong, Laura? You sound a bit edgy. You didn't have any problems, did you?'

'Only one,' she sighed. 'Your half-brother confronted me, of all people.'

'Daniel!' He made the name an explosive sound, his fingers jerking convulsively on the wheel. 'But he's supposed to be in France. What's he doing over here?'

'You tell me. You're the one he's come to see.'

'Oh, hell!' He raked his hand through his hair. 'That's Mother's doing, you can bet on it.' He grimaced, changing gear as they moved out on to the main road. 'I thought when she went to France for the summer I'd be OK for a while, but she must have enlisted Daniel on her side. Damnation!'

He revved the car into action and put his foot down on the accelerator. 'She never gives up, you know. First it was my exam results she was hassling me over. Why hadn't I worked harder, didn't I realise I should have to take my place at Warwick's one day? Push, push, all the while.'

Laura hated to hear the bitterness in his voice. She said, softly, 'Perhaps you're not aware of your own potential, James. You got through your exams without even trying. What could you achieve if you set your mind to it?'

'What would be the point in that?' he interjected with a scowl. 'I can't see why Daniel insisted on my coming to university in the first place. I'm interested in art; that's my forte. I want to do something creative with my life, perhaps dabble in design, not play second fiddle to my brother in the family business. As if there could be room for anyone else at Warwick's, with him holding the reins.' His face was tight with resentment. 'I could have gone to Europe, or the States, done something interesting, instead of wasting four years studying. It's not as if my degree will get me a good start in the firm. He means me to work my way from the ground up.'

The car shot along the road, eating up the tarmac at a frightening pace.

'Slow down, will you?' Laura demanded, clutching at the leather upholstery.

'I'm sorry,' he said, easing off. 'I don't mean to take it out on you. I just feel as if I'm being got at from all directions just lately.' His mouth jutted in a familiar way. 'Mother went on and on when I sent the bill home for the car. It wasn't my fault, the bend was too tight and the road was slippery, but to hear her on the phone you'd have thought I was twelve, not twenty-three.'

'I imagine she was worried about you,' Laura pointed out drily.

James made a face. 'I suppose you're right,' he agreed with a sigh. 'I should have gone home to Oakleigh last Easter. That would have made her feel better, but I didn't, and now she wants to know what kept me, who I was with, etcetera, etcetera, as if the whole dynasty was going to fall apart.'

'Easter?' A line etched itself between Laura's finely arched brows. 'But you stayed on here—we went on that picnic—why didn't you tell me that you were expected at home?'

'Oh, come on, Laura. You had been depressed for a long time, and it was hardly surprising, what with your father, and then all the business worries. Someone had to see you through it.'

'You did it deliberately, because of me? Oh, James—I didn't know. You said your plans had fallen through.' She felt totally wretched at having caused him trouble with his family. She might do all she could to avoid Daniel Warwick, but James was her friend, like the brother she had never had. Now she was consumed with guilt. 'For your sake, I wish you had gone home,' she said quietly.

'It makes no difference.' James shrugged. 'I'd only have been nagged about my lifestyle. It was much more fun, being with you. It's bad enough

that Daniel has control of my money till I'm
twenty-five, without my being accountable for
who I spend my holidays with. I don't see why I
should put up with having my friends vetted as
well.'

Laura tensed. A drum-beat started up in her
ears, drowning out the sound of the car's engine.
She said, slowly, 'You really think that's why he's
here? You think he'll try to find out about us?'
Her mouth tightened at the thought.

'That's probably the size of it.' James concentrated on the road ahead, taking a left turn into
Laura's street.

'But you'll tell him that he's on the wrong track,
that there's nothing between us?'

He pulled up outside the brick building which
housed her flat, switching off the ignition. 'Isn't
there?' he said huskily. 'I like you a lot, Laura,
you're very dear to me, you know. You've stood
by me, helped me out, always been there when I
needed someone. That means a lot to me.'

'James, I'm your friend, you know that—but I
don't want you to get the wrong idea—I——'

He cut her short, placing a finger over her lips.

'It's OK, Laura, I know how you feel, you don't
have to say anything. Let's leave it for now.'

She bit back what she had been about to say,
but it didn't stop her from being troubled. James
had been her friend, since the day he had walked
into the shop, looking for a painting for his

mother's birthday, and she had chatted to him, and shown him around, not knowing that he was related to Daniel. She didn't want him to think that there could be anything more; she had never felt that way about him.

'James. . .'

He said firmly, 'Don't worry about it. And put Daniel out of your mind. I'll handle him.' He rested one arm along the upholstered door-panel. 'I don't suppose he'll stay around for more than a day or so, anyway. He doesn't get to spend a lot of time at Oakleigh. His London apartment is more convenient to him as a base for operations.'

Laura forced herself to remain calm. James had a point. It was unlikely that she would ever meet up with Daniel again, so she had no reason for being on edge. She was overwrought, that was all.

'Don't forget about the barbecue down on the beach tomorrow,' James reminded her as she slid out of the car. 'I'll pick you up around seven if that's OK?'

'That's fine,' she said, but really she didn't feel that anything in the world was fine any longer. It had been a nerve-racking day, one way and another.

CHAPTER TWO

THE party was being held on a sheltered part of the beach, where the sand was flat and firm, and the rocky coves and inlets made a fitting background for a smugglers' get-together. A fire burned smokily in a circle of grey stones, and the crashing of waves mingled with the music from several strategically placed radios. Someone had mixed a bowl of punch that was going down well.

Laura looked for Maggie among the crowd, but there was no sign of her. Something must have delayed her—she still had not returned from her assignment when James had arrived to pick Laura up, and she had left a note suggesting that they meet out here.

She shifted restlessly, trailing her bare feet over the sand, making little runnels with her toes, while she sipped at her drink. Walking down to the water's edge, she found a craggy seat where she could sit and watch the sea breaking with small ribbons of foam against the shore.

Taking out a small sketch-pad from her bag, she began to outline the long, curving sweep of the bay, her pencil moving with swift, sure strokes over the paper.

Daniel's appearance in her life had left her deeply unsettled. He had always had that effect on her, though, from the very first time she had seen him.

She had been on vacation from college, helping out in the shop one day, when he had walked in and his tall, commanding presence had seemed immediately to fill the room. His hair was dark, almost jet-black, crisp and well cut, framing a tough, strong-boned face. It was a disturbing face, Laura had decided. The jaw was determined, uncompromising, the mouth hard, a hint of ruthlessness about it. She had suspected that he would make a formidable opponent, should anyone be foolish enough to get on the wrong side of him. His clothes were casual, but obviously expensive, and they had done nothing to disguise the lean, muscular fitness of the body beneath.

He'd said, without preamble, 'I'm looking for Calum Brant, is he about?'

She stiffened at the note of authority implicit in his voice, then said, 'He's out at the moment. Can I help you at all?'

She came out from behind the counter, and his cool grey eyes followed her movements, sweeping over her in a swift, appraising glance that took in the skimpy T-shirt, and the denims that clung faithfully to the rounded curve of her hips. She found herself resenting that thoroughly male assessment.

'You must be Laura,' he surmised thoughtfully. 'I'm Daniel Warwick.'

She nodded, and said, 'You're from Oakleigh Manor, aren't you? My father said that you would be coming here.' Calum hadn't told her what their business was about, just that Warwick would be calling. He had seemed preoccupied, weariness causing his shoulders to sag a little, and she had thought he looked paler than usual. She couldn't be sure why, but she had the impression that this meeting was one he would rather avoid, though she knew better than to question him just yet. He had been snapping all morning—he wasn't a man who knew how to share worries. 'He's gone to look at a Regency card table, but I dare say he won't be too long.'

'It's doesn't matter. I managed to get away rather earlier than I expected.'

He began to move around the room, inspecting what was on show, and she asked, 'Are you interested in antiques?' Her hand rested on a finely crafted cabinet, and now she ran her fingers delicately over its panel of intricate inlaid work.

'That would depend on the piece in question,' he said. He glanced around briefly, his gaze dismissive. 'It appears your father has an interest in paintings. Is there anything worth seeing?'

Laura recalled the conjecture over the remarkable Warwick collection, and said tautly, 'I'm afraid you won't find any Monets or Renoirs in here,' adding, 'That would be more your style, wouldn't it?'

'Would it? What makes you think that?'

Shrugging, she said, 'Only what I read in the papers.'

His grey eyes took on a glinting, feral quality. 'You really shouldn't believe all you read.'

She regarded him levelly. 'Which bits would you have me ignore?' she murmured, and his mouth twisted in acknowledgment of the thrust.

She gestured to the far wall. 'We do have some pleasant studies in oil. This one, for instance, was painted about fifty years ago.' The subject was a sailing-ship, its cargo shrouded, being tossed on black, stormy seas, much as it might have looked in the days when contraband silks and brandy and spices were brought to shore under cover of darkness.

He studied the painting carefully. At last, he turned back to her and said, his tone quite bland, 'Is it the subject that appeals to you, or the finer techniques employed by the artist?'

'You obviously have no romance in your soul,' she muttered. 'You don't see anything that you like particularly, do you?' she said, frowning.

'Do you?' he countered.

'We stock the kind of thing that most people want,' she argued, irritated that he should put her on the defensive. 'We have to make a living.'

'I doubt you'll make it with this stuff.' He

walked into the ante-room and Laura followed,
eyeing him moodily. Her father did all the buying;
maybe it wasn't top quality, but he had kept his
business going for years. How dared Daniel
Warwick come in here and imply he was doing it
all wrong?

He was studying the painting that occupied a
prominent place on the far wall. Daniel Warwick
was supposed to be a connoisseur of art; just what
would he make of this one? she wondered with a
scowl.

The signature would give him no clues. Her
mother had signed it using her maiden name,
Castell, so he would not be able to connect it with
Laura's family.

It had been painted in France, a landscape of
little white cottages that tumbled down to the sea,
where sailing-boats rocked gently on the waters,
the evening sun casting its rays over the harbour
wall. It was all she had left, a tangible reminder
of her mother, and she would cherish it for ever.
She braced herself, waiting for his reaction.

He said slowly, 'Now this is more like it. There's
an incredible amount of feeling here, it reaches
out to you, as if the artist knew the place inti-
mately, and loved it.'

Laura felt a reluctant glow come to life within
her. She alone knew how much her mother had
cared for the little fishing village where they had
lived for only a few short years.

'There are so few Jane Castell originals,' Daniel murmured.

Laura said quietly, 'She died young—who knows what she might have achieved if only she had lived?'

He stepped back to take another look at it. 'How much is your father asking?' he said suddenly. 'It's uncanny—hard to take in all at once. I spent several summers in France, in my youth. My stepmother has a house out there, on a hillside overlooking the sea, and whenever I had the chance I used to walk down to the harbour and look at the boats.' He turned to Laura. 'This is so like the place where I stayed, it could almost be the same village.'

'It isn't for sale,' she said, her throat tight. All her mother's work had gone now, except for this one, and Laura would make sure that this was here to stay. Calum Brant had never forgiven his wife for leaving him and taking their daughter with her. After her death, he had gone over to France and had brought Laura back to England with him. All the paintings had been sold, except this one, which had been a gift to Laura from her mother, and nothing would persuade her to part with it.

Daniel said, 'I'm sure he would reconsider if I made it worth his while. . .'

The look she gave him was full of irony. 'Even you could never offer enough to buy this,' she gritted. 'Jane Castell was my mother, you see; that makes the painting priceless.'

'Your mother?' he echoed, his interest sharpening. 'Do you have any more of her work?'

Laura shook her head. 'No. That's the only one.'

He looked back to the painting. 'Pity,' he said. He turned to her then, transferring his gaze to her slender form. For the first time since he walked into the shop, he smiled, and the effect was sensational, making her heart miss a beat. He said softly, 'It's a great shame it isn't for sale, you know, because, apart from that painting, there's only one other thing in the shop worth going after.' His glance moved over her, pausing to dwell disconcertingly on the soft, full curve of her mouth, and she edged away from him, a deep flush of pink riding her cheekbones.

Calum walked into the shop just then, the jangling of the bell jarring the silence that had fallen, and she hurried forward, disturbed to see him looking grey with fatigue.

'Any luck with the table?' she asked, and he answered shortly,

'None at all, complete waste of a journey.'

'Oh, dear.'

He looked past her to where their visitor stood, and said, 'Warwick. I'm sorry if I kept you waiting.'

'Not at all. I arrived early. Laura has been showing me around.'

Calum nodded. 'Have you had coffee?'

'We've been talking,' Daniel said, and Calum turned to Laura with a frown, so that she excused herself and went into the kitchen.

She felt as if she had been dismissed, while the men talked business, and that annoyed her, but it was her father's way, and she had become used to it over the last few years. At least being at college much of the time gave her a breathing space and helped her to get things into perspective.

After that first day, Daniel became a regular visitor. He had some connection with her father's suppliers, she learned, although his own interest lay in property development.

Whenever he came by the shop, he made a point of seeking out Laura, and, despite her misgivings, she found herself looking forward more and more to those times. He could be a very persuasive man when he set out to charm, she discovered. It was not long before just a glimpse of that dark head or the sound of his deep, well-modulated voice was enough to quicken her pulse and send her temperature soaring.

He asked her out, and eventually she agreed to spend an occasional evening with him. He would take her into the local town for dances or to the cinema, or perhaps they would enjoy a meal together. They were pleasant, light-hearted dates, but she was well aware that he would have taken things further, given the chance.

Laura was always too wary of getting deeply involved with him to allow that to happen. Her father was guarded when he spoke about Daniel, and she could not rid herself of the notion that, somewhere, something was not quite right. Her loyalties were torn, and she had to keep a tight rein on her feeings. Already, Daniel had her emotions see-sawing out of control, though she tried not to let him see the effect he had on her. In a great many ways, he was much more experienced than she was, and she was increasingly reluctant to expose the true extent of her innocence and naïveté to his scrutiny.

It was difficult. She could not stay immune indefinitely to his gentle, teasing manner, and the long, lively conversations they had only deepened the attraction he held for her. She began to wish that the sun-filled days might never end, because that would mean she would have to go away, back to her studies, and surely that would be the finish of everything, of all her secret hopes and dreams. Of course he would forget her once she had gone back to college. She was just a young woman, devastated by the eruption into her life of a dangerously attractive man.

Calum's health was her biggest worry, however. He tired very easily these days, and, though she did her best to encourage him to take things a

little more slowly, there was often a strained look
about him, a bluish tinge to his lips that caused
her to watch him anxiously. She wondered if
Daniel's visits upset him, but when she asked what
prompted the meetings between the two men he
was strangely reticent.

Then, one day, he said shockingly, 'He wants
the shop, hadn't you guessed? He thinks he can
persuade me to sell, and I sometimes think that
he doesn't much care how he goes about it. But I
won't give this place up. This is my whole life, it's
all I know. I'm not going to let it go without a
fight.'

She had paled, doubts crowding in on her mind,
but she said slowly, 'Why would he want it? It
isn't his style, surely?'

'Warwick isn't drawn by the property,' Calum
gritted. 'Whatever he might say, it's the site he's
after. There's a great deal of potential in it for
anyone with enough money to carry out the
development.' He threw her a swift, searching
look. 'Did you think he was interested in you?' At
her silence, he pressed his lips together. 'I'm sure
he likes you, Laura, but you have to bear in mind
that there's probably more to it than he's letting
on right now. Think about it. He has all the time
in the world, and if he can use it to win you to his
side he'll have an ally in the opposite camp.'

She made a small sound of negation, and he

added thoughtfully, 'On the other hand, if anything more permanent were to come of your liaison with him, it could work to our advantage.'

Her father's words left Laura deeply troubled. She pushed to the back of her mind his last, almost calculating remark. He was not well, and the pressures of running the business were increasing week by week, so that he was not his usual self. But how could she have forgotten that Daniel, too, was a businessman first and foremost; he hadn't acquired his hard-hitting reputation out of thin air, had he? He was powerful, wealthy, with a solid background of high-achieving ancestors, and she had been crazy even to entertain the thought that she could belong in his world.

From now on she would have to take extra care to batten down her wayward feelings or she would surely be destroyed. Deliberately she set about building a wall around herself, distancing herself from him, so that she could not be hurt.

It was not an easy thing to do. Aware of the new and unaccountable coolness that had crept into their relationship, Daniel treated her with a cautious familiarity, refusing to be put off by her reservations.

He found her in the garden behind the cottage one heat-hazed morning, and stood watching silently for a few moments as she trimmed the roses. His steady gaze unnerved her. She said, 'You'll find my father in the shop.'

He frowned at her cool, clipped tone, but answered quietly, 'He's dealing with a customer. I can wait.'

Laura turned back to the roses, fixing her attention, dropping the overblown heads into a bucket. She heard him move, and steeled herself as he came towards her.

'OK,' he said, 'let's have it. What's this all about?'

She gave him a blank look. 'Roses,' she said, 'what else? They need tidying if they're to look their best.' She snipped at a bloom and a shower of waxy pink petals floated to the ground.

Daniel's hand closed over hers, his other reaching out to pluck the secateurs from her fingers. Placing them on a ledge, he turned back to her.

She said slowly, 'I hope you're good at waiting, because he won't sell, you know. It might be only bricks and mortar on a prime piece of land to you, but this is our home. He's put a lot into it over the years and I can't see him settling anywhere else, so you might as well give up now and concentrate on your other sites.'

He eyed her speculatively. 'Sometimes people can't see what could be for their own good. They need a push in the right direction.'

'And you've set yourself up as the Almighty?' Her voice was tight. 'What are you planning to do, bulldoze us into the earth and erect a monument to another Warwick victory in our place?

Aren't you content with all the trophies you have dotted about the country already? Not to mention your overseas projects,' she added darkly.

His brows came together. 'How much has your father told you?' he asked.

'What else is there to tell?' she countered harshly. 'Isn't it enough that you want to take his livelihood away? Or has he got hold of the wrong idea? Tell me you aren't interested in the property, and I'll believe you.'

'I can't do that, Laura. But there's no need for you to be concerned——'

'No need!' she echoed incredulously, her lips parting in pained astonishment. 'You're making my father ill with all the worry about selling up. It's got to stop, do you hear me? I won't have you harassing him any longer, Daniel.'

'If your father's anxious, it isn't because of my offer,' Daniel denied firmly. 'In fact, it could be the answer to all his problems, except that he's too stubborn to see it. He won't listen to reason.'

'I don't think I care much for your idea of reason,' Laura ground out through her teeth. 'You've just admitted it—you're planning to whip my home from under me, and you imagine I'll accept it without a murmur? What kind of idiot do you think I am?'

'Laura, it isn't the way it seems—I wouldn't do anything to hurt you. Lord help me, I'm crazy about you. . .' He ran a finger along the smooth curve of her cheek, a light, fleeting caress, but she gasped, his touch searing her skin like flame. Calum had said he would try to use her to further his cause if he could. Was that what he was doing now? She couldn't bear it. . .

'Don't,' she said jerkily. 'Don't do that.'

Daniel's mouth tightened. 'I hadn't realised you found my touch so distasteful,' he rasped. 'My apologies. It won't happen again.'

Hurt and angry, Laura clamped down on the sharp retort which sprang to her lips, and ran into the house, almost colliding with a bewildered Calum in her rush to get away.

'I heard raised voices,' he said, frowning. 'What's going on, Laura? What were you two arguing about?'

'Just clearing the air,' she muttered fiercely. 'Nothing for you to be anxious about.'

'I don't want you fighting with him, Laura,' Calum said. 'We need him on our side. He could make or break us, and all we have to hope for is his goodwill. Without it, he could make life very difficult for us.'

She froze. 'What do you mean?' she said huskily, her throat suddenly very dry.

'I mean, the way things are going, his feelings for you are just about all there is between me and bankruptcy. Don't rock the boat, Laura. You could do a lot to make our future look a whole lot brighter. Do I have to spell it out?'

She stared at him in disbelief, unable to take in immediately what he had just said. Daniel came in through the open patio door, and Calum said quickly, 'Laura's a bit on edge these days; you shouldn't pay too much account to the vagaries of women's moods.'

Laura gasped, the light dismissal of her feelings like a blow to the stomach. Her stunned gaze flickered over Daniel's implacable features, then she turned and made her escape from the suffocating confines of the room. She was so angry that she wanted to smash things. It was only the thought of Calum's drawn, pale face that kept her from lashing out at the pair of them. She could not guess at the demons which drove her father. Something was badly wrong; there was a lot Calum was withholding, and it hurt to know that he had not felt able to trust her with the truth.

'Why?' she said, later, when she was alone with her father in the small living-room. 'Why is it so important that we keep on the right side of him?'

Calum winced. He sat hunched in his chair; he looked suddenly old and very tired. 'I owe him money,' he said at last, stiffly. 'A lot of money. More than I can find, now or in the next few years. He isn't pushing for it, but he could. At any time.'

Laura clenched her fingers in her lap. 'I don't understand. Why did you have to borrow so much? The shop is mortgaged and you had enough capital for the rest. Trade isn't that bad, is it? How has it happened?'

Calum lifted a shoulder in a helpless gesture. 'I thought I was doing everything right, but somewhere along the line I made some wrong moves. Warwick made me a loan.'

'Why didn't you tell me?' she said raggedly.

He grimaced. 'I thought I could handle it.'

He had always been introverted, wrapped up in his own world, excluding her. In part, she put it down to the fact that he had lived alone when her mother left him to go to live in France, taking Laura with her. Perhaps he had never come to terms with that separation.

Over the next few days, though, he talked more to her about business matters than he had ever done. It was clear that the tension of coping with money problems was still gnawing at him, but at least a lot of things had been brought out into the open now, and he was sharing his problems with her. She knew that some of the bills had not been paid, some of their usual suppliers had not sent goods that had been ordered. Stocks were running low.

He came into the ante-room one morning as she was inspecting the frame of her mother's painting, debating the best way to repair a chipped corner. He passed a jaundiced eye over the painting, throwing a couple of brown envelopes on to a low table.

'More bills?' she queried sympathetically, and Calum grunted a reply. He was preoccupied, staring at the picture, his brow furrowed.

'The recession's biting hard, people are just not buying these days.' He sighed heavily. 'I need a source of money, fast. My credit rating is low, getting lower all the time, and the wholesalers won't give me the items I need until the accounts are squared up.'

Hesitantly, Laura said, 'But—doesn't Daniel know the people you deal with? Isn't he on friendly terms with them?'

Calum shifted restlessly. 'Oh, he knows them all right. But as to whether he would help, that's another matter.'

'Have you asked him?'

He shook his head. 'I can't be sure of his reaction. It may make matters worse. After all, it may suit him to see me being squeezed out. That way, I might have to sell up all the sooner. He might get them to apply an even greater stranglehold.'

Calum's words kept returning to Laura as she worked on her chores throughout the rest of the morning. Daniel had made no secret of his wanting the property, but surely he would not be ruthless enough to deliberately harm her father in order to achieve his own ends? Yet, how could she be certain of that?

The question gnawed at her continually. Even

as she made her way into the town after lunch it was foremost in her mind.

It was not a good day for shopping. The oppressive heat had been building up for hours. The air was heavy with it, the sky darkening ominously with the threat of the storm to come. The bus trundled along the roads, picking up passengers at every stop, until the temperature inside was stifling. Opening the window to its full extent did nothing to help. Laura fidgeted in her seat, relieved when at last they arrived at the centre. Thunder rumbled in the distance. She wanted to finish her shopping quickly, and get home before the rain started, but the heat sapped her energy, draining her, along with the dark, troublesome thoughts that haunted her mind.

The first droplets came as she left the marketplace; a gentle, welcome respite, but it wasn't long before the clouds burst and the rain began in earnest, pouring from the heavens in a steady, drenching stream, hissing over the ground. She was soaked before she reached the bus terminus, water dripping from her hair on to the upturned collar of her jacket.

A car drew up alongside her and she passed a casual glance over it, watching the rain sluice across the gleaming metalwork. Daniel said curtly, 'Get in, Laura.'

She hesitated and he rasped, 'Hurry up, we're blocking the flow of traffic.' He pushed the door open, and she climbed in, depositing her bags on the floor at her feet.

'Where are you headed—home?'

She nodded, and he swung the wheel, steering the car out into the road. 'Am I taking you out of your way?' she asked, and he jerked his head in denial.

'I have to see your father.'

It was not a comfortable journey. For the last week, when they had gone their separate ways, it had been marginally easier to damp down her feelings for him and relegate them to a secret corner of her mind, but having him beside her in the close confines of the car left her far too vulnerable. Daniel did not speak and Laura was too conscious of his proximity to be able to relax. She was only too aware of the assured movements of his strong brown hand and wrist as she went through the gears. Unwillingly, her gaze transferred to his tough, masculine frame, and skittered away almost immediately. Her limbs were tense, restless. She did not like the effect he had on her. It took away her peace of mind, leaving her exposed, defenceless.

He brought the car to a halt in front of the cottage shop and she hastily unclipped her seatbelt and reached for her bags, anxious to get away from him as quickly as she could. His fingers brushed her legs fleetingly as he pulled on the handbrake and she jumped at the contact, her skin over-sensitised by the fevered wanderings of her mind. She looked at him in alarm. Daniel's mouth made a grim line, his eyes glittering with swift anger, and she swallowed hard, turning to let herself out of the car.

Calum wasn't around. The shop was closed for the afternoon, and she guessed that he had probably gone to a local sale that he had mentioned earlier.

'I doubt that he'll be too long,' she told Daniel, showing him into the living-room. 'I'll just get out of these wet things and then I'll see to some coffee.'

He didn't answer, but looked her over with cold curiosity, a muscle flicking in his jaw. Laura decided on a hasty retreat.

In the kitchen, she went over to the sink and filled the kettle, frowning into the water as it gushed from the tap. Even now, faced with his coolness, she could not believe that he meant them any harm, but the uncertainty was tearing her apart.

Waiting for the water to boil, she set a tray with cups, cream and sugar, looking up with a start as Daniel walked into the room.

'Did you want something?' she asked, pausing with the cream jug in her hand. Her voice sounded very brittle.

'Several things spring to mind,' he said drily,

looking her over, 'but I doubt you'd be inclined to comply.'

A startled rush of colour ran along her cheek-bones. To hide her confusion, she put the jug down, and continued with the small tasks of seeing to the coffee. Daniel made a restless movement, glancing down at his watch. 'Is he likely to be much longer?' he said brusquely. 'He was expecting me, and I don't have a great deal of time. I'm supposed to be somewhere else in an hour.'

'I shouldn't think so,' Laura said. 'Anyway, the coffee's ready now. Won't you stay for a cup?' She sat down at the table, and after a moment he came over and took a seat opposite her. Her lashes flickered as she pushed a cup towards him. 'Was it important, your reason for seeing him today?'

He shrugged. 'There's no desperate urgency, I suppose. I dare say the world will continue to revolve in the usual way.'

Laura's mouth made a wry twist. 'You're prepared to play a waiting game?' Was she part of it, as her father had hinted?

'I'm in no hurry. I'm not getting worked up over it, and I fail to see why you should, either.'

She spooned sugar into her coffee, adding cream. 'But then, it isn't your home that's at stake, is it?' she pointed out carefully. 'No one wants to come along and demolish Oakleigh, do they?'

Daniel's jaw clenched. 'You ought to know that your father's living in a fool's paradise. He can't afford this place; it's a millstone round his neck. I'm sure that sooner or later he'll come to realise the truth of what I'm saying.'

'Perhaps you're right,' she murmured. 'But he isn't well, and I think that trying to make this place succeed is all that's keeping him going right now. Do you and I have to become enemies over it? Can't you make things a little easier for him?'

'"Enemies" is putting it rather strongly, wouldn't you say? But tell me what you had in mind, won't you? After all, the ball's in your court. It seems to me that you're the one dishing out all the cold-shoulder treatment.'

'That isn't true,' she protested, chewing at her lip.

He threw her a scornful glare. 'You have to be kidding,' he grated. 'The slightest touch from me and you go into deep freeze like an affronted virgin. I should have thought we'd gone past that stage by now. I thought we could be friends, at least.'

'Would it make a difference?' she said huskily. 'To your plans, I mean?' Her eyes were wide, glimmering softly, and he stared at her, brooding, one long finger tracing a path around the rim of his cup. She did not think he was going to answer, and she said quickly, 'Everything's so unsettled. My father isn't as strong as he was, and I worry about him.' She stiffened, a shadow crossing her eyes. 'Can't you help him, Daniel? He's going through a bad time just now.'

'What do you imagine I can do?'

'You're on good terms with his suppliers, aren't you? Couldn't you talk to them, persuade them to give him a chance to get back on his feet?'

He frowned, and her spirits plummeted. Then he said, 'It's possible, I suppose. I might be able to arrange something.'

Laura breathed a sigh of relief. 'Thank you,' she said, her smile tremulous.

Daniel's expression was serious. 'Don't thank me, I haven't done anything yet. And it will only stave off the inevitable, you know. Sooner or later your father will have to come to terms with the fact that he's gone in over his head.'

She acknowledged the warning with a grimace. 'At least it's a start,' she said flatly. 'When do you think you'll be able to talk to them?'

He pushed his cup away and got to his feet. 'It will have to be within the next few days. I'm leaving for Switzerland shortly, and I don't expect to be back for some time. We've a number of projects in Europe that I have to oversee.' He walked towards the door. 'I've appointed an agent to see to matters here.'

Shock held her rigid. She ought to have known that sooner or later their ways would veer apart, but it was something she had not wanted to think about. Now, the suddenness of his disclosure hit her full force.

Slowly she stood up. 'You're leaving,' she repeated dully. 'How long will you be away?'

He shrugged. 'Who knows? It could be a couple of years, or more. I may even decide to stay over there.'

She felt as if she had been winded, the pain growing in her chest, constricting her lungs. Surely this was a dream, some horrible kind of nightmare?'

'Does my father know?' she said hoarsely, but as soon as the words were uttered she knew that he couldn't, because he would surely have told her, given her some kind of warning.

She started towards Daniel, dazed, like a sleep-walker who did not know where he was going, or what he was doing, but who was bound all the same to keep moving.

'I haven't told him,' Daniel said. His eyes were dark and unfathomable, his face unsmiling, only inches away from her own. 'Does it. . .' he paused '. . .make a difference?' There was a faint tinge of irony underlining his words but she paid it no heed. How long would it be before she saw him again? In these last, heady weeks of summer he had made such an impact on her that it had seemed he had changed her whole pattern of existence. When he went away, it would be as if the sun had gone out of her life for ever.

'Laura?' he murmured questioningly, and she moistened her lips which had suddenly become very dry. Her glance was drawn to the angular line of his jaw, and she could see the fine pores of his skin, the devilish cleft in his chin that was so attractive. She caught the whiff of some subtle, elusive fragrance, and her gaze drifted, compelled, towards the firm contours of his mouth. Hesitantly, she lifted her hands up over the fine, smooth silk of his shirt.

'I didn't know you were thinking of going,' she whispered. 'You didn't say. . .'

His dark brow lifted. 'Should I have? I hardly thought you would be interested, you've been so cool of late.'

She gave a little moan of denial, pressing her fingertips gently to his mouth. 'I'm sorry,' she said huskily. 'I was so anxious about my father. . .' She broke off, searching his features intently as her fingers absently explored the firm line of his jaw. He was stiff, unyielding. She could feel the tension in his body like a taut wire, and it tore at her to know that they might part in this cool, polite manner. 'Can't you understand?' she whispered. Her fingers crept up to wind themselves in the crisp, dark hair at his nape, and she moved closer, leaning into the hard, muscled wall of his chest. She was still for a moment, revelling in the contrast of his hard strength against the softness of her curves, his warmth penetrating the thin fabric of her blouse with shocking sensuality. Her breasts firmed, burgeoning against his chest.

His breath caught. She heard its swift intake, and wondered at the effect she was having on him. His fingers slid over the small of her back, and a swift, unbidden ripple of pleasure shook her. His thighs tangled with hers, a heated, flash-fire contact, and her body arched, meshing with his. She was intoxicated by him. She looked up, saw the stunned, stark glitter of desire reflected in his eyes, and for a blinding moment she was heady with the power that came from pure feminine instinct, the knowledge that stemmed from Eve.

'Daniel. . .' she whispered unevenly, and it seemed that his dark head bent towards her. His mouth seemed achingly close and her lips parted in trembling invitation.

'How could I resist?' he muttered, his voice roughened. 'You're pure, sweet temptation.' His thumb brushed lightly over the soft, vulnerable curve of her mouth, then his lips descended to make their own unhurried, tender exploration. Her body was suffused with warmth, a heavy languour pervading her limbs.

His lips shifted, marking out a honeyed trail of kisses along the silken column of her throat. 'I've waited so long, Laura,' he groaned against her hair, 'I've dreamed of holding you like this.' She melted into the seductive invitation of his arms, a soft, shuddery sigh escaping her as his fingers stroked with tantalising sureness over her breast.

Then, bewilderingly, he moved back a little, staring down at her, his eyes dark, intense, his mouth firm, beautifully moulded. Her eyes widened in confusion. His steady scrutiny of her was disturbing, and she began to wonder if she had done something wrong. Perhaps he found her naïve, too young and inexperienced. He had spoken of temptation, but she wanted desperately to be more to him than just a passing whim. Wasn't she fooling herself? How could she ever hope to become part of his life? He moved in the world of high finance and corporate deals; she could never belong there.

He drew her back towards him, his mouth seeking hers, his hand shaping her thigh. 'I want to make love to you, Laura,' he muttered thickly, urging her closer to his strong, hard body. When he would have deepened the kiss, though, she pulled back, uncertain, overwhelmed by her own intense awareness of him, afraid of his experience, terrified that he might mock at her innocence.

Daniel felt her withdrawal. He said, 'I thought this was what you wanted, too, Laura? Just a few moments ago, you were telling me, if not with words. Could I have misread the signs so badly?'

'You're going too fast for me,' she muttered, her tone bleak. 'I wasn't thinking straight; I don't know why it happened.' Her small teeth pulled at her lip. 'All I know is that it isn't right for me. You're going away, and I don't think I can cope with a casual affair, a one-night stand. That's what you're offering, isn't it?'

'What were you expecting?'

Laura stared at him blankly. 'I don't know. . .' she said, her voice unsteady. 'You caught me unawares. . . I wasn't prepared. . . Something more than a quick fling before you went away, I suppose.' There was an edge of bitterness to her words. That was all that she meant to him, after all. A flirtation, a pleasant way to pass a few hours before he left, nothing more.

'And if I hadn't made up my mind to go away, what then?' he gritted softly. 'Would that have changed the situation?'

She did not know how to answer that. Many of her friends at college were much more liberal-minded than she was, and would be amazed that she even had to take time to think about Daniel's suggestion. Unhappily, she mumbled, 'I'm not sure. I always believed there should be some kind of commitment between people before—before they——'

'—went to bed together?' Daniel finished for her. 'What kind of commitment did you have in mind? Marriage?'

He bit the word out, and her head jerked back at the ice in his tone, as if he had slapped her. 'Do you have something against the institution?' she asked in confusion.

'For other people, no. For myself, I've learned to my cost that a woman may have various reasons other than love for wanting a ring on her finger. I'm a wealthy man. That hadn't escaped your notice, had it, Laura?'

'I hadn't thought. . .'

She broke off, looking at him in dismay. His eyes had darkened to a chilling grey slate. 'Hadn't you?' he demanded harshly, his mouth a hard, tight line. 'I had almost convinced myself that you might prove to be genuine, but you knew exactly what you were doing, didn't you? I put you on the spot, telling you that I was leaving and you panicked. You thought you had to act quickly.'

'What do you mean?' she asked shakily, the colour draining from her face. He was like a stranger to her, threatening her with the cold menace of his voice. Why was he so angry with her? What had she done?

He stared at her with glacial dislike. 'Whose idea was this—yours or your father's?'

'I don't understand,' she protested. 'What does my father have to do with any of this?'

His jaw clenched. 'Don't act the innocent with me. I heard what your father said to you that day, after we had been out in the garden—he didn't need to spell it out, did he, Laura?'

Her eyes grew large, horror dawning in them,

and she began to shake her head. His lips curled in derision at her mute protest.

She whispered, 'It wasn't——'

He cut in savagely, 'You decided there and then what you were going to do, didn't you? You thought you had plenty of time to work up to it.'

'No. No—I don't. . . I don't know what you mean,' she stammered.

He smiled nastily. 'Don't you? For weeks you've blown hot and cold with me, till I didn't know whether I was on my head or my heels. You flinch away at my slightest touch, yet now, all at once, you can't get close enough. I wondered at your father's delaying tactics, when the only obvious thing to do was sell up. What was he hoping for, Laura? What were you both hoping for?' He flung her a glare, then bit out, 'Don't answer that—I know what you wanted, well enough.'

'You don't understand,' she said huskily. 'I—you're going away—I wanted—I'm going back to college, and I thought——'

'You thought this was your last chance to set you and your father up for life,' he ground out, balling his hands into fists, and she took a faltering step backwards, frightened by the pent-up violence she recognised in him. 'You calculated I'd be so crazy for you that I'd agree to anything, even marriage. Well, I'm telling you, you fouled up,

Laura. Too bad, the act failed. Your little seduction plan might have worked, sweetheart, except that it's been tried before, by experts.'

'You're making a mistake,' she said hoarsely and he laughed, but it was a harsh sound—there was no amusement in it.

'No. My mistake was that I didn't figure out your game right away. I was blind. I let my guard down and you crept in.' He moved swiftly to the door and wrenched it open. Turning, he said tightly, 'I don't like to be used, Laura.'

The slam of the door rocked her on her feet. She stared sightlessly at the oak panels, his words reverberating through her head like slow, painful drum-beats.

CHAPTER THREE

LAURA had no clear recollection of the week that followed. All she could be sure of was that it was all over, and that somehow, unbelievably, the end had been her own fault. No. . .it had been a mistake; Daniel had misjudged her and condemned her, and that was what really hurt. He had not been prepared to listen to reason, because the prejudices of his past blinded him to the truth, and how could she fight that?

Some friends invited her to stay with them for a few days, and she accepted, glad to get away from the cottage shop. If she had moped about the house, her father would have been bound to ask what was wrong, and she could not bear to go into explanations just then.

On her return, she found Calum studying his ledgers, a deep frown etched into his brow.

'How's it going?' she ventured, anxiously. She did not know what damage she might have caused after the argument with Daniel. In trying to make matters easier, she had probably succeeded in causing a complete catastrophe.

'It isn't good,' Calum muttered, running his pencil over a page, 'but it could be worse.'

Laura sighed wearily. How long could they go on before the crunch came? It was too early to know whether Daniel had spoken to the suppliers about their credit rating, and she could only hope that he had not been provoked into seeking bitter retribution. His anger had been swift when he thought she had set out to beguile him into helping, but it was also deep-seated and that made her increasingly apprehensive.

Her unease grew as she walked into the ante-room. At first, she could not place the cause of her anxiety; there was only a strong feeling that things were not the way they should have been. Puzzled, she looked around, her gaze drawn to the empty place on the wall where her painting should be, and for a moment she stared at the bare patch, her throat closing in dismay. Then common sense took over. Of course, there was a simple explanation. Her father must have removed it in order to repair the damaged frame. She went in search of him.

'My painting,' she began, 'it isn't anywhere that I can see—have you put it away for some reason?'

Engrossed in his work, he gave no sign that he had heard, and she repeated her question. At last he dragged his attention from the figures he was totalling, and stared at her blankly.

'Mother's painting,' she persisted. 'Did you put it in the workroom?'

Carefully, he put down his pen, and she bit her lip with impatience.

He said heavily, 'I've sold it, Laura.'

Her jaw dropped in shock. Then she shook her head at him. 'You're joking,' she chided. 'Of course you are. You wouldn't have done that, would you?' She gave him a weak, cajoling smile. Of course he wouldn't have sold it.

Calum did not return her smile, and she stared at him, dumbstruck.

'I had to do it, Laura,' he muttered. 'You'll come to see that I had no choice. You know how bad things are, don't you? At least the money from the sale will keep us going for some time. There was no other way.'

'No.' She gave a strangled cry. 'I don't believe you. You couldn't have. You know how much it means to me.'

'Yes, I do know, Laura.' His expression was bleak. 'But we can't live in the past for ever. Life is for the living.'

She looked at him, ashen-faced. 'You don't understand,' she whispered brokenly. 'You'll never understand, will you? Mother had a gift, a talent that only comes to a few. Her work meant everything to her, but you couldn't face that, could you? That's why you gave her an ultimatum, and you never forgave her for the decision she made. You couldn't bear it because she went away.' Her voice shattered.

Calum got to his feet wearily. 'You're upset right now. You're not thinking straight. Otherwise you would see that I had no option but to sell the painting.'

Laura fought against the growing constriction in her lungs. 'There is always an alternative, there has to be. But you didn't want to take it. You wanted to get rid of that painting. It was always a thorn in your side.' With the back of her hand, she dashed away the mist of tears that sprang to her eyes. 'She was my mother, and you can't make me shut her out of my life as if she had never existed.'

She rushed over to the bureau where the sales record book was kept, and pulled open the drawer. 'I'll have to get it back. Who did you sell it to? Is there a phone number?'

'You can't do that, Laura,' Calum said tiredly. 'It's too late.'

'It can't be. Who bought it? I'll ring them up and explain the situation.'

Her father averted his eyes. 'It was Warwick,' he said quietly. 'He told me he was prepared to pay whatever I asked for it. It was the one thing of real value that we had. I couldn't refuse, I was desperate.'

Laura reached for the support of a chair, her limbs suddenly boneless. 'Oh, God,' she whispered. 'It can't be true. Not him, of all people.'

She stared despairingly at Calum. 'How could you?'

He made no reply, and she said carefully, 'We'll give him back the money he paid. I'll give up college and get a job straight away to help out.'

'It's no use,' Calum said. 'The money's gone, or most of it, anyway. I used it to pay off some of the debts, but I still owe Warwick the full amount. As it is, it's all I can do to hang on to the property, but Warwick said he would take the painting and give me a breathing-space over the loan.'

Laura buried her head in her hands. Daniel had bought her painting, knowing that she would never have willingly parted with it. He knew how much she treasured it, and yet he had made certain that she would not be able to get it back without ruining her father. He had done it deliberately, vindictively, in order to inflict as much pain as he could. She had not realised how deep his hatred of her went, but now the taste of it was bitter in her mouth.

She straightened up, her fingers twisting in the fabric of her skirt. Daniel thought he had won this battle, but the war was only just starting. One way or another, she would get her painting back, even if it took her a lifetime.

In the meantime, her father would need her support.

* * *

Laura shivered as the breeze from the sea buffeted her. Darkness had fallen like a grey mantle while she had been sitting here, and now she was aware of the noises all around her, of the crackling of the fire that had been made of driftwood, of the laughter and snatches of conversation that floated on the air currents.

She looked down at the sketch she had made, and crumpled it into a tight ball in her fist. Lifting her hand, she threw the paper far out into the water, then sat back and watched as it was snatched up by the tide, buffeted by the choppy waves until it disappeared from view.

She stood up, and began to walk along the beach, skirting the water's edge. The sand shifted behind her, and pebbles scattered. Looking round, Laura saw James and Maggie coming towards her and waved a greeting.

'Have you only just arrived?' she asked, and Maggie nodded, coming to walk beside her.

'The flight was delayed,' she explained. She seemed a little breathless, as if she had been hurrying. With her flowing black hair and dark-eyed, vivacious looks, it was no surprise that she was always in demand for modelling assignments that took her all over the world.

'Now that you've arrived at last,' James said, 'we can take the party on to the yacht. Don't go empty-handed, though. You can carry a bottle or two. I'll round up the others and show them the way.'

Laura regarded him with suspicion. 'You never mentioned owning a yacht,' she said quizzically.

James gave her a lofty stare. 'A man is allowed some secrets,' he murmured.

When they reached the quayside, it was too dark to make out more than the shape of the yacht, but it was certainly among the largest of the craft that swayed gently on the moon-silvered water.

On board, Laura was taken aback by the luxury of it all. The fittings were of deeply polished wood and brass, and upholstery that was sheer invitation. It made her nervous to even think about wine-spills. She kept a careful hold on her own glass.

'How did the assignment go?' she asked Maggie as James showed them into the galley. 'Did you get time to go and visit your brother and his family?'

'I did. For once, there were no hitches, so I had more free time than I expected, and John and Kelly were able to show me around.' Her eyes sparkled. 'They managed to book an early flight, so they'll be arriving some time around dawn. It's going to be crowded, you know—are you sure you don't mind them staying at the flat?'

'Of course not,' Laura said quickly. It would be chaotic for a while, with John and his wife, plus their two small children, but she added, 'Anyway, as I told you before, I'm due for a break, and I've made up my mind to take off somewhere for a while.'

Maggie helped herself to a slimline tonic. 'I noticed your cases were packed. Michelle and Sarah asked you to go and join them in Spain, didn't they?'

Laura nodded. 'I'm not sure that's quite what I want, though. I thought I'd drive somewhere for a change of scene and book into a quiet hotel.'

James put in, 'What's this about a hotel? You could come and stay at Oakleigh for a while, and enjoy the countryside. You said you'd take me up on my offer some time—well, now's your chance.'

Someone caught Maggie's attention, and she slipped away quietly into the saloon.

James said, 'What do you say—we could take the yacht along the coast tomorrow, and be at Oakleigh for lunch.'

Laura thought about it. 'I'm tempted,' she murmured, 'but it wouldn't do much to improve Daniel's frame of mind, would it? If he's already on the lookout for problems it could just tip the scales and put you right out of favour.'

'Too bad.' James studied her over the rim of his beer can. 'Don't concern yourself about Daniel. I doubt that he'll be there. He usually lets our housekeeper know if he's going to be staying, but Heather hasn't had word from him. And, from what I gather, he's over here to negotiate for a lucrative new development—one of the biggest he's ever gone after, so it's most likely that he'll be operating from his London base. It's a real hush-hush deal, one that he's wanted for a long time, and from the sound of it he's going to be too tied up to be worrying about what I get up to.'

Laura digested that. The prospect of going to Oakleigh certainly held an appeal. James had always talked about the old house with affection, and it was in the heart of beautiful, open country-side, just the sort of place to relax in. But if she was truthful with herself, it was the possibility that she might come across her painting which attracted her to the idea most of all. After the sale of the shop she had put in an offer through Daniel's agent to buy it back, but there had been no reply. Her brows met in a frown. Somehow, she had to find a way to get it back.

James misinterpreted her hesitation. 'Why shouldn't you stay at Oakleigh?' he demanded. 'Even if Daniel is there, it doesn't matter. It's my home, too, and I'll invite who I want. Just because Daniel was born into it, doesn't mean he has to have everything his own way.'

The resentment was back in his tone, and Laura wondered if he would ever adjust to the circum-stances of his birth. Being the younger half-brother grated on James, that was why he kicked over the traces when he had the chance.

In a way, though, James had a point. Why should she let thoughts of Daniel Warwick spoil her life? Hadn't he already caused her enough pain and heartache?

'I think,' she said slowly, 'that I should very much like to spend a little time at Oakleigh. Thank you.'

James grinned and gave her a hug. 'That's my girl,' he chuckled, and flipped his can into a bin that was already beginning to overflow with empties.

It was the early hours of the morning before the party began to break up. The galley, Laura noticed, trying to smother a yawn, was littered with glasses and plates, and the remains of food.

'Why don't you go and curl up in the main cabin?' James suggested. 'I'm going to run Maggie over to the airport to meet her brother's plane, and then I have to pick up some of my things from the university. There's no point in dragging you along there as well.'

Maggie agreed. 'You won't get much sleep back at the flat, with John and Kelly and their brood arriving. I can let James have your cases, if you want to stay on here.'

'Well, if you're sure. . .' Laura conceded doubtfully.

James went off with Maggie to the car, and Laura looked around at the devastation that used to be the galley. Morning would be soon enough to deal with that, she decided. Right now, she was deadbeat, and the thought of bed seemed like heaven.

In the large main cabin, she stepped out of her clothes, leaving on her peach-coloured satin teddy. She washed quickly, then climbed into the wide bed, sinking with a gratified sigh beneath the cool sheets. It was not long before the gentle lapping of water against the sides of the boat had eased her into a deep, exhausted sleep.

Some time later, she moved restlessly, rubbing at her eyes with her knuckles. She blinked, fighting with the tangle of bedclothes, and stared around at her unaccustomed surroundings. The door stood open, and she squinted at it in puzzlement for a few moments. Surely she had closed it? Then light penetrated her fogged brain and she realised that James must have come back. Stretching her limbs, she closed her eyes for a few blissful seconds.

'Up to your old tricks, Laura? You never know when to give up, do you?'

The deep, gritty voice shocked her into instant wakefulness. Jack-knifing to a sitting position, she stared, wide eyed, at the long-limbed figure of a man who lounged against the doorjamb.

It was unfair, she thought, a mute wail strangling in her throat. He had no business being here. James had said. . . But it was Daniel. There was no doubt about it. Unless he had a double.

'Are you deliberately following me around?' she demanded tautly, shooting a glare in his direction.

'I might ask you the same question,' he retorted coldly. 'I came here in order to find a modicum of peace and quiet, and instead I find you waiting for me. Don't you think it's a little late in the day to try that again? I'm hardly likely to fall for the same ploy twice.'

'You're paranoid,' she said flatly. 'I always suspected it. Now I know for sure.'

He scowled darkly. 'What, exactly, are you doing in my bed?'

Laura's head went back. She swallowed hard. 'Don't you mean—James's bed?' she ventured slowly.

Daniel's eyes narrowed on her. 'So that's how the land lies, does it? I might have guessed. You don't believe in missing opportunities, do you, Laura?'

'I don't know what you mean.' Her voice was low and troubled. There was something in the way he was looking at her that had her alarm system on red alert.

'I take it that you are the woman he has been spending all his time with these past few months?'

Laura shrugged. 'We see each other occasionally.'

His glance swept over the wide bed. 'That much is obvious,' he said with heavy sarcasm, and Laura felt her skin prickle with irritation.

'You're making assumptions,' she said tightly, flashing him a look of distaste.

'Shouldn't I?' he rasped. 'You outlined it for me with your own lips, the other evening. He's the one who's going to be very wealthy, isn't he, Laura? That's why you're seeing him.'

'No. I like James,' she insisted heatedly. 'We're friends. Even you can't make anything bad out of that.'

'Can't I? You're forgetting—I know you, Laura. I know all about you and your idea of friendship.'

He spat the words out and she was stung to retort, 'At least James is human, with warm, human emotions; he's not a block of ice, like you.'

'Is that how you think of me? I wonder how you came by that idea?'

His steel-grey eyes raked her mercilessly, and she clamped her lips shut, dragging the duvet to herself with shaking fingers, her heart thudding erratically against her rib cage. Her protective gesture brought a derisive curve to his hard mouth, and her fingers clenched spasmodically on the sheet. She hated the way he made her feel. It was not fair that he should put her on the defensive every time they met.

He came towards the bed, leaning over her, and

Laura shrank back against the pillows. His light-weight jacket brushed against her arms.

'Modesty? Why bother?' he asked, with a sardonic lift to his brows. The leaping glitter of his grey eyes filled her with apprehension, then turned to acute panic as he bent closer, trapping her with his arms, one on either side of her, his palms flattened on the bed.

'Am I making you nervous?' he enquired with silky menace. 'Isn't this what you wanted?' His finger slid over her shoulder, naked except for a thin silk ribbon which he deftly hooked to one side. Angrily she slapped at the offending hand, but that was a mistake, because although it had the effect of making him remove his fingers, it also meant that she lost her grip on the sheet, and his dark head shifted slowly. Her skin began to burn where his gaze lingered.

She said stonily, 'Have you always been given to flights of fantasy, or is this a neurosis that came with puberty?'

He straightened, threatening her with his height, and said through his teeth, 'When did your mercenary instincts come scrabbling to the fore—at birth?'

'Another delusion,' she remarked, her mouth making a grim line. 'What a pity you have such a complex about wealth. I dare say that it's the only thing that you have to offer a woman. She'd certainly wither away if it was charm she was looking for.'

'Whatever it is that you're looking for,' he muttered fiercely, 'you had better remember that I'm on to your game. If you're waiting for James to feather-bed your life, I'm telling you now, you're in for a long wait. Your boat will come in when the Sahara floods.'

She opened her mouth to tell him what she thought of his high-handed, insulting manner, when a sudden onset of rocking disturbed the yacht. A clattering followed, and Daniel said with cool contempt, 'The lover returns, I presume.'

Laura glowered at him. 'I'd like to get dressed. Will you get out of here?'

He ignored her, his attention turning to James as he came into the room with Laura's cases. Putting the luggage down by the bed, James said, 'What are you doing here, Daniel? You're supposed to be in London, aren't you?'

'Never mind that,' Daniel snapped, directing an icy glare towards the cases. 'What's the meaning of those?'

James shoved his hands into his pockets and gave his brother a truculent stare. 'What does it look like? We're obviously going somewhere. Does that bother you? Do you think we're about to elope?'

'That would turn out to be the biggest mistake you ever made in your life,' Daniel ground out.

'That's true,' James said grimly. 'Which is why we're going to do things properly. I've invited Laura to spend some time at the house, so that she can get to know the place better. The Oakleigh diamond would look good on her finger, don't you agree?'

'What!' Daniel's explosive reaction made Laura jump. She looked at James in dismay. What on earth had possessed him to say such a thing? He was being deliberately provocative, throwing petrol on the fire. If anything was calculated to make Daniel see red, it was the thought that a penniless outsider with no background might seek to become part of the Warwick empire. The only event that could have been worse was that the outsider should also be herself. Being James's paramour was one thing—belonging to his family was a different matter altogether.

Having dropped his bombshell, James made for the door, saying casually, 'Well, I don't know about anyone else, but I'm starving. I'm going to cook up some breakfast, then we can get under way.'

Daniel stared furiously at his departing figure, an angry red stain darkening his cheekbones. Laura worried at her lip with her teeth, biting the sensitive skin, when he pounced.

'You think you've been very clever, don't you?' he rounded on her, flaying her with the knife-like glitter of his eyes. 'Why this family? Weren't there any other rich young bloods you could make a play for? Or was it a deliberate choice? You didn't get very far with me, so you turned your attention to James, getting back at me with a double-edged sword? He's easier to work on, isn't he? It didn't take much to get him to fall into your trap. One flash of those big green eyes and he was already halfway there.' His eyes slitted. 'Don't think you've won. You might well have made first base, but your days are numbered. I'll see to that.'

Laura did not reply. The rage inside him blazed like a furnace, and anything she said would only have been consumed in the flames. His every word insulted her, and her anger was equal to his. She would not allow him to intimidate her. She would go to Oakleigh with James, and there she would look for her painting. Only when it was back in her safe keeping would she be satisfied, and Daniel could burn in a hell of his own making.

CHAPTER FOUR

'THAT was a close thing,' James said, as they sped along the main road towards Oakleigh. 'I've never seen Daniel so near to blowing his top. Still, at least he's on his way to London now. We can relax.'

For how long, though, Laura wondered, pulling a face. 'I can't think what possessed you to do it,' she muttered crossly. 'First you let me think the yacht I'm staying on is yours and it turns out to be his and——'

'I keep an eye on it while Daniel's away—that makes it as good as mine, doesn't it?' James demanded, his chin jutting belligerently.

Laura sniffed. 'Presumably this diamond you mentioned is some kind of heirloom?'

James nodded. 'An extremely valuable ring—promised to the very next Warwick bride.' He gave her a wolfish grin. 'I thought he was going to explode, didn't you?'

'He'll most probably go and find himself a wife within the month just to scupper your plans,' Laura said, with a frown. 'How do you expect him to react when you throw that kind of statement at him out of the blue?'

James sighed, hunching his shoulders. 'I know, I know. But he annoyed me. He's no business interfering—although I suppose, to be fair, he's only looking out for me. He's had his share of nasty moments where women are concerned—that Jennifer Ryan business hit the newspapers and I don't think he ever quite recovered from that episode.'

A knot formed in Laura's chest. She did not want to think about Daniel and his women friends, past or present. Especially present, a little voice murmured inside her head, and she quelled the thought instantly. Whatever she felt for him belonged in the past. It had long since been destroyed. 'I remember reading about it,' she said in a low voice. 'She's an actress, isn't she?'

'Mm—Daniel was knocked for six when they met,' James told her. 'She's a real beauty. . .on the outside. Not so pretty when things started to go wrong between them, though.'

Laura's fingers clenched in her lap. Even after all this time, she could recall the pain and unhappiness that had enveloped her when things had gone wrong for herself. Why did it still hurt so much? Daniel didn't mean anything to her, did he? She would not let him under her skin.

'We're home,' James announced, sweeping through a wide entrance on to a long, gravelled drive. Laura glanced around, and as her gaze took in the magnificent yellow stone building, a soft sound of wonder escaped her lips. It was the most beautiful house she had ever seen. A broad swathe of fine green turf fronted it, in turn bounded by mature oak-trees.

James led the way through an arched doorway, topped by the family crest, into the entrance hall, where a couple of highly polished tables were adorned with huge flower arrangements.

A dark-haired woman came to greet them. Her face was a smooth oval, with a wide, smiling mouth, and bright, amazingly blue eyes that reflected the smile.

'Heather,' James said, 'I'd like you to meet Laura Brant. She'll be staying with us for a while.'

'Daniel phoned to say you were on your way. It's good to have you back with us.' Heather turned to Laura. 'I'm pleased to meet you, Miss Brant. I hope you enjoy your visit.'

'I'm sure I shall,' Laura murmured politely. 'Do call me Laura.'

'I expect you'd like to freshen up after your journey,' the older woman said. 'Shall I show you to your room? I could bring you a tray up there— it's a while yet till the evening meal.'

'That would be nice, if it's no trouble.' Laura suddenly realised that she was famished.

James said, 'I'm going to pop out to the stables and say hello to Grey Lady. I'll introduce you later, Laura, if you like.'

'Thanks, I should.'

'I'll see you in a while, then.'

A curving staircase opened out into the hall, and Heather guided her up, past portraits of people who, Laura guessed, must be Daniel's ancestors. Her trained eye noted that all the paintings were well-preserved—even the frames had been carefully chosen to blend to perfection. Everything about Daniel's home was clean and bright, obviously well cared for.

Her room was no exception. The theme of soft green and gold was picked out in the deep-pile carpet and floor-length velvet curtains. Even the luxurious duvet reflected the tranquillity of the colour scheme.

'Your bathroom is through there,' Heather said, indicating a door in the far wall. 'You should find most things that you need. If not, give me a shout and I'll see what I can do.' Glancing around, she added, 'I see that Tom has brought your cases up. He's my husband—he acts as caretaker, odd-job man; you name it, and he does it. There's a groundsman, and there are a couple of stable-hands as well. You'll soon get to know everybody.'

'Have you and Tom been here long?'

'For as far back as I can remember. We wouldn't want to work anywhere else. The family have been good to us.' She went over to the door. 'I'll leave you alone for a while to settle in.'

When she had gone, Laura began to unpack her

clothes, shaking them out and hanging them in the roomy wardrobes. Her fingers stilled on the dress she was holding. Had she made a big mistake coming here? Doubts were beginning to creep in, now that she was in Daniel's home. Even though he was miles away by now, she could still feel the vibrations of his anger, and she felt more and more like an intruder. What had seemed like a good idea to begin with was rapidly starting to wane in appeal.

What was she afraid of? she asked herself. After all, it wasn't as though she had done anything wrong. From way back, any problems had been of Daniel's own making. Besides, he could hardly cause her any harm from London, could he? More than likely she was worrying unnecessarily. Even so, she could not prevent a shadow of apprehension from crossing her mind. Instinctively she recognised that Daniel was not the kind of man who would let matters rest as they were.

Giving herself a mental shake, Laura decided on a quick shower, and a change of clothes. She had to do something to break out of the strange mood that had descended on her. It was odd, but it must be this lovely house that had stirred her to melancholy reflections.

Thoughtfully, she picked out an attractive dress that was simply styled, in a delicate blend of several different shades of blue. The fabric was soft, and faintly clinging, with a skirt that flared slightly from the hips. She found herself wondering whether Daniel would like the way she looked, then her cheeks burned, and she pushed the errant thought from her mind.

Daniel hated her. Any attraction that sparked between them had been extinguished by his mistrust and suspicion. Jennifer Ryan and others like her had a lot to answer for in their eagerness to get on in the world. Maybe they thought Daniel Warwick could be their stepping-stone to success. He mixed with all the right people, and he was seen in the best places. But it was Laura, in the end, who suffered for their ambitions.

In front of the oval mirror at her dressing-table, she applied a quick, light make-up, brushing her eyelids with shadow, and adding a delicate touch of blusher to her cheeks. She finished off with a spray of perfume, then sat back and looked at her reflection critically. It would have to do.

Dinner was at seven, James had told her, and it was not far off that time now. She began to make her way down the splendid wide staircase. Seeing James burst in through the front door in his usual exuberant fashion helped to dispel some of her qualms.

He stood very still on the bottom step, looking up at her. 'Now there's a sight to welcome a man home,' he grinned. 'You look good enough to eat. Blue suits you, Laura. Is that a new dress?'

She laughed down at him. 'No, it isn't. You've

seen it before, dummy. Anyway, I feel as if I should be wearing satin and lace and long, swirling skirts in this house. Something more in keeping with the historical vibes.'

'Hmm. . .' James looked thoughtful for a moment. 'Satin and lace would look good on you—the skimpy variety, though, that's more to my taste.' He came towards her, leering devilishly, like a brigand, and swooped suddenly, catching her around the waist and lifting her up. She gave a little squeak of protest, then collapsed in gurgling laughter as he rolled his eyes and made wicked suggestions against the soft material of her dress.

'Wretch,' she chuckled, beating at his shoulders with her hands. 'Put me down.

'Never, fair lady——' he growled, 'not until I have had my evil way with you. . .' He swung her around, and it was then that they both saw Daniel crossing the hall.

For a heartbeat she stayed, poised in mid-air, then James let her down, dropping her in an untidy heap on one of the lower steps, with a muttered, 'Oops! The devil is on my tail. Wonder what he's doing back here. I'd better dash.'

He shot up the stairs, calling out, 'Shan't be two secs, got to change.'

The shock of seeing Daniel left Laura immobilised against the wooden rails. She groaned inwardly. Hadn't she foreseen something would go wrong? She might as well pack her bags now.

Daniel was dressed very formally in a grey, waistcoated business suit, and he was carrying a bulging briefcase. Laura stared at him, her eyes round and disbelieving. 'You're not in London,' she said, accusingly, scrabbling behind her for a wooden support and missing.

'Obviously not,' Daniel said curtly.

Laura tried sliding her back up the newel-post, struggling against the sudden weakness in her limbs. She said, breathlessly, 'How long will you be staying?' as if he were the visitor, and not she.

He treated her to a wintry smile.

'For as long as it takes,' he told her. 'I shall work from here. It's less convenient, but that isn't of great importance right now.'

Laura missed her footing, and slid down the remaining two steps as her legs gave way beneath her. She tried desperately to regain her balance by grabbing on to the nearest rail, but landed instead in an ungainly sprawl on the floor at his feet.

Daniel looked down at her with dislike. To her shame, she discovered that her skirt had ridden up, and she was showing an inordinate amount of smooth thigh. With shaking fingers she attempted to put matters right, and found that the material was somehow wedged beneath her and was resisting all her efforts. Daniel said something unpleasant under his breath and his hand shot out, closing around her wrist in an iron grasp, pulling her unceremoniously to her feet.

She moistened her dry lips, keeping a wary eye on him the whole time. His grip on her was bruising, but he did not let her go and she would not give him the satisfaction of knowing that it hurt. He dragged her towards him, his face very close to her own, his mouth a hard, grim line. The taut menace of his body dispelled any flickering hope that he might have had a change of heart over the last few hours.

'What is important,' he mouthed tightly, 'is that any plans you might be hatching are smothered from the outset, and that is why I'm back, make no mistake. I'm here to spike your guns, Laura, don't you forget that.'

The rigid, uncompromising angle of his jaw emphasised his determination and almost succeeded in unnerving her. Almost, but not quite. She must never let him see that he was getting to her. She clung to her conviction that she was in the right, and answered with a defiant toss of her head. 'Don't try to threaten me,' she said, clamping her teeth together. 'Let's dispense with the melodrama, shall we? If you want me out of your house, just say so, and I'll leave.'

'Oh, no.' His mouth twisted nastily. 'You'd like that. That would be too easy, wouldn't it? You'd go, and James would be after you like a shot. I'd be cast in the role of big, bad brother, and you'd be the sweet innocent. No way. You're staying right here, where I can keep an eye on you.'

She brushed an imaginary speck from the bodice of her dress. 'Whatever you say. It's of no matter to me whether I stay, or whether I go. Your hang-ups are entirely your own business. They really don't concern me.' She looked at him directly, and there was ice in her gaze. 'One other thing,' she added, with a coating of frost, 'I don't appreciate being manhandled. Please let go of my wrist.'

He laughed softly. 'Oh, I do remember that, Laura. You want marriage first, don't you? Sorry we can't oblige.' He jerked her hand away from him and walked up the stairs, leaving her shaking with rage and humiliation.

They were playing a cat-and-mouse game, with Laura as the victim, and his unyielding confidence made her grind her teeth. She was unused to this kind of skirmish, to a battle of wills with an adversary as skilled as Daniel Warwick. She did not know the rules, and even if she did, she suspected that he would not play by them.

She eventually found the dining-room, off the hall, through panelled double doors. It was bathed in the soft amber of evening sunlight that streamed in through full-length leaded windows, which curved to allow for the inclusion of burnished wooden seats. Plump cushions were scattered invitingly on the polished surface, and Laura thought wistfully how pleasant it must be to sit there and look out over the stone-walled terrace at the sloping sweep of the gardens.

'They're called lovers' seats.'

She gave a nervous start. She had not heard Daniel come up behind her.

'Care to try one?' he asked silkily, baring his teeth.

Her lashes flickered. 'No, thank you. I think I prefer the sofa.'

His smile was sardonic. He had discarded his jacket, and had changed his clothes for cream, smoothly fitting trousers, teamed with a tan silk shirt, the top few buttons open, so that she was disturbingly aware of the sun-bronzed column of his throat. He came towards her, his stride rangy, relaxed, yet deceptive, because there was no disguising the lean, threatening vitality.

She slid down on to the couch, and averted her eyes so that she did not have to take note of the mocking glitter evident in his own.

Her glance travelled over the exquisite furnishings, the opulent rugs that covered the floor. 'This is a beautiful room,' she said softly.

He inclined his head in acknowledgement. 'Some of the pieces in here have been in the family for generations, like the escritoire, over there, but there are one or two items that I came across on my travels that I felt would fit in.' He ran a hand along the smooth surface of a book-case, filled with an assortment of titles in embossed leather bindings.

Laura wondered bleakly if her mother's painting could be included in that statement.

'Do you think you'll find your room comfortable?'

'Yes. It's perfect, thank you,' she said in a stilted voice.

'Good. I asked Heather to prepare that one specially.' A faint smile pulled at his mouth, and it bothered her, that smile, because she did not know what was amusing him. But then, she admitted, she had never been sure how his mind worked.

James came to join them then, and they went over to the table. Laura tried to do justice to the beautifully cooked food that Heather presented, but really she did not feel like eating. She was too conscious of Daniel the whole time, remembering too well the warmth of his fingers like a steel clasp on her arm. Remembering other times, when his touch had stirred her senses beyond reason. Why did he have this effect on her? No other man had ever made her feel the way she did. It was unfair, she reflected. The one man she had every reason to avoid seemed to hold a powerful, magnetic attraction for her. A dangerous attraction.

'What's this new deal you're working on now?'

James asked Daniel, as he helped himself to vegetables. 'Something important, I gather.'

'A new leisure complex,' Daniel answered. 'A lot of people are interested in getting the contract, so it's a question of the most exciting ideas combined with a reasonable quote for the job. The competition will be fierce. It'll take a lot of thought, some innovative design work.' He gave his brother a reflective glance. 'You might be interested in taking a look at what we've come up with so far—you might have some ideas to contribute.'

James paused momentarily, his hand coming to rest on his napkin. Indecision flickered across his features. Daniel's readiness to involve him so soon in the family business had obviously come as something of a shock, but, from the faintly hopeful gleam which crept into his eyes, it was not an unwelcome one. Thoughtfully, he murmured, 'I'd like to do that.'

Daniel gave a satisfied nod. 'Come along to the study after dinner, if you want. I've only two or three weeks to get to grips with this project, so I mean to start straight away.'

'Fine,' James said, then hesitated. 'Laura——'

'That's OK,' she said quickly, 'I brought some reading material with me. It'll give me a chance to relax and catch up with myself.' James looked relieved, and Laura smiled to herself. She saw through Daniel's strategy. If he'd thought she was going to whine and make a fuss, he had read her wrong. But hadn't he always?

'We've a well-stocked library, if you'd care to use it,' Daniel invited, 'or maybe you'd like to get one of the stable-lads to saddle you up a mount. The estate is fairly extensive; you might enjoy a roam around it—so long as you allow yourself time to return before it gets too dark. We wouldn't want you getting lost on your first day.' Briefly, she glimpsed his teeth, very white, very even.

Oh, wouldn't he? Laura thought with irritation, but she acknowledged the offer with as much grace as she could muster. He was not only devious, but clever with it.

Shortly after the meal was over, the two men went and shut themselves in the study, poring over the numerous documents which Daniel had brought back with him from his London office. Laura did not take up the offer to ride, but she did wander into the library and pick through the vast selection of books. Selecting a novel by a well-respected thriller writer, she took it over to an armchair, and curled up for the evening. If her attention wandered occasionally, she ruthlessly dragged it back. Daniel would not win.

Darkness fell outside, and after her third yawn in a matter of minutes she closed the book, deciding to call it a day. Turning into the corridor, she halted a moment to get her bearings, then made her way to her room.

On the wall beside her door there was a painting of the house, made in an earlier century, before the later additions and renovations had been made, and she stopped to study it. A tread sounded on the carpet next to her, and she turned to see James coming towards her.

'Is this the room you've been given?' he said, frowning.

'Yes,' she said, a little puzzled by his expression. 'It's delightful.'

'Hmm. You're finding your way around all right, then,' he said. 'It's a large house. It can be a problem to begin with.' He stood beside her, relaxed, one hand pressed flat against the wall. 'This part of the house is designed in the form of an L—my bedroom's around there,' he gestured with his head, 'in the other half of the L, next to the room my mother uses when she's at home.' He sighed. 'It's good to be back here, you know. I'm only just getting used to the idea that all my studies are over, that the summer is in front of me.'

He leaned towards her, his voice low and husky. 'I'm glad you're here with me, Laura.'

Looking at James, Laura knew a pang of anxiety. He was watching her in a way that he had never done before. His eyes were half closed, and there was a strange, intent darkness within them.

She wondered unhappily whether she ought to have applied the brakes in their relationship sooner. It had not occurred to her that things might be getting out of hand; she had always thought of James as she would of a brother—as a friend.

'It's a new experience for me, staying in a place like this,' she murmured. He smiled, moving closer, putting his hands either side of her. His head bent towards her, and she was not sure what to do, how to react. He had never kissed her before, other than a quick, light embrace, and she knew that was not what he had in mind now. Somehow, she would have to get things back on a normal footing. She would have to let him down gently, but quite how she was to go about it she was uncertain. She moved her head slightly, so that James's lips just brushed her cheek, and then she stiffened. She had not heard Daniel approach, but now she saw him. His face was dark, his features harsh in the lamplight.

'Laura?' James whispered, turning to see what she was staring at, and then he, too, saw Daniel, and pulled away from her, but not before she had felt the sudden tensing of his limbs.

'Goodnight, James,' she said quietly. 'I'll see you in the morning.'

He cast a brief glance at Daniel. 'Goodnight, Laura.' He touched his mouth gently to her forehead, then he moved away in the direction of his own room.

Daniel's expression was frozen, like ice in a bleak winter landscape. She walked to her door, unhappy about the tension that had sprung up with such suddenness between the two men. For it was there, hanging in the air like a knife about to descend.

Pausing with her fingers on the handle of her door, her gaze lifted once more to Daniel, then she looked away quickly, biting her lip at the cold cynicism that tilted his mouth.

Alone in her room, she washed and changed for bed, slipping into a cool nightdress that left her shoulders bare except for narrow, lacy straps. She picked up her hairbrush and stroked it through the tawny length of her hair, frowning unseeingly into the mirror. Why was James acting so strangely? They had known each other for so long, and there had never been this tension between them. She would have to do something to set things back on an even footing before. . .

A clatter, followed by a muffled crash, sent her startled gaze in the direction of the sound.

For the first time, she noticed a door, partly hidden behind soft brocade curtains. Curiosity took her towards it. There was no key, and she turned the handle, pulling it open.

Daniel swore under his breath. He finished picking up the remains of a plant pot, while Laura simply stood, gaping at him, the hairbrush still in her hand.

'What are you doing here?' she said, aghast.

He stood up, putting the broken pieces to one side and brushing the dust off his hands. 'I live here,' he said tersely. 'This happens to be my room.'

His hair was damp, as if he had just come from under the shower. He was wearing only a towel around his midriff—his chest was bare, his bronzed skin gleaming faintly. She dragged her gaze from his supple body, forcing her attention back to his face. Her mind skittered, working feverishly.

'But—you can't—it wasn't—there's no key,' she stumbled.

'Of course there's a key,' he rasped. He went over to a washbasin, and began to rinse his hands. 'But I don't intend to go looking for it right now.' He spoke as if she was acting in a hysterical fashion. Yet being confronted unexpectedly with the stunning evidence of his powerful, vital masculinity at such close quarters, knowing that he was using the room right next to her own, had left her completely shaken.

'It hadn't occurred to me that. . .that the rooms were next to each other,' she muttered unevenly.

'And that thought obviously bothers you,' he said with a sardonic twist to his mouth. 'Had you hoped James might visit you later tonight?'

His glance ran over her, from the fiery mass of her hair, over her slender shape outlined by the flimsy cotton of her nightdress, to her bare feet peeping out from under the hem. 'He won't, you know. Why do you think I put you in the room next to mine? But I'd hate to deprive you. . .' He paused, bringing the lazily sensual grey gaze to rest on her flushed face. 'Perhaps I can make amends. . .'

He had caught her to him before she had time for evasion, kissing her with a thoroughness that made her dizzy. She beat at him with her palms, but it made no difference—the kiss went on, and on, and his hands closed over the rounded swell of her hips, pulling her towards him, so that the softness of her curves collided with his hard, lean body in a shattering explosion of sensation. The thin material of her nightdress made her vulnerable to the searching, arousing touch of his fingers. Her blood pulsed through her veins with a wild, surging excitement that shamed her, as the gentle coaxing of his hands and lips elicited her body's trembling response.

He brushed his mouth over the smooth, supple line from throat to bare shoulder. Then he held her at arm's length, running his gaze over her slender form.

'I don't want you,' she said fiercely, unable to stop the shaking of her body that was echoed in her voice.

'You never did. Perhaps I went about things the wrong way.' His hands shaped her breasts, and she bit back a little moan of despair as she felt the aching nubs flower against his palms.

'No!' She wrenched herself free with a choked cry, and took an unsteady step backwards, watching him the whole time, her eyes wide with uncertainty.

'I should have offered you the Oakleigh diamond,' he said. 'That would have changed your mind.' His mouth curved, he seemed to move, and she delayed no longer.

She turned and fled into her own room, shutting the door between them and leaning against it, as if the strength of her slender body could keep him back. Her heart had set up a loud discordant thudding, and his soft laugh mingled with it, coming through the thin barrier between them as if he was just a heartbeat away.

CHAPTER FIVE

LAURA came awake slowly the next morning, hazy snatches of dreams flitting with tantalising elusiveness across her mind. She moved restlessly in the big bed, stretching her limbs wearily in the soft, smothering depths of the bedcovers.

Propping herself up against the pillows, she cast a frowning look around the unfamiliar room, still shrouded in the grey light of dawn. Memories began to come back to her, and she sat up properly then, all thought of sleep vanishing in the blink of an eye.

It was real, after all—she had not imagined everything. She was here, in Daniel's house, and he was just a whisper away from her. Involuntarily, her fingers closed on the sheet, hugging it close, a swift rush of heat invading her cheeks.

Thinking of him, in the very next room, was enough to galvanise her into action. Sliding her legs out of the bed, she pulled on a robe and headed for the bathroom. A shower would help her to shake off the bewildering, honeyed images that had threaded her dreams. She must not let him get under her skin this way or she would be lost.

A short time later, she made her way downstairs, into the breakfast-room. Her throat constricted as she saw Daniel, already seated at the table by a window, helping himself to coffee from a ceramic jug. He glanced up as she came into the room, a glimmer in those dark eyes, and Laura's body tensed, alert and wary.

James walked in from the kitchen, carrying a plate of toast, and munching on a slice.

'Stoke up,' he said cheerfully. 'There's bacon, eggs, mushrooms—Heather's a wonderful cook.'

Laura's stomach rebelled at the thought of food. 'Just toast will be fine, thanks.' She seated herself at the table, carefully avoiding looking at Daniel.

'I thought you might like a ride over the estate after breakfast,' James suggested, his glance sliding with approval over her jeans-clad figure. 'I always ride first thing in the morning when I'm at Oakleigh. It sets me up for the day.'

'It sounds like a good idea,' she said.

James looked pleased. 'When we get back,' he said to Daniel, 'I'd like to take another look at those designs you were showing me yesterday. I came up with one or two options that you might like to consider. . .'

'Fine,' Daniel said. 'I'll expect you later.'

It was clear that after a night's sleep James was in a better frame of mind than he had been on the previous evening. He and Daniel must have cleared the air between them, for the present at least.

The days that followed took on a similar pattern. Laura and James would ride first thing, and then she would amuse herself sketching, or visiting the local beauty spots, while James was closeted with Daniel in the office.

Daniel's study was always littered with paperwork. She was passing by the open door one afternoon when James waved her in, and Daniel started to gather up the pile of documents, putting them into folders.

'See that these planning documents and cost estimates are always locked away,' he said to James as she walked in. 'We don't want confidential material left lying around.'

'Will do,' James said, sliding an arm around Laura's shoulders. 'Sorry I've been so busy,' he murmured in her ear. 'I'll make it up to you. I thought we might go out later, into the town, perhaps?'

She nodded agreement, and he said, 'I'll have to go and get cleaned up. I'll catch you later, OK?'

Daniel flicked a contemplative glance over her as James went out. 'Getting bored already?' he asked, a glint of mockery in the dark eyes.

'On the contrary,' she answered stiffly, annoyed by that cynical appraisal. 'I needed a break, and so far it has been just what I wanted.'

Daniel clicked the top on his pen and leaned back in his chair. 'James has been really taken with the plans for the leisure complex. He has a lot of sound ideas, and he needs time to get them down on paper before the closing date. I hope you understand that, because if you had hoped he might be free to entertain you, you're going to be disappointed.'

'I can make my own amusement,' she said. 'I don't need James to hold my hand.' A note of sarcasm crept into her voice. 'It does seem to bother you, though, that I have time to relax. In fact, I'm surprised you haven't found me something to do. I'm sure you must have paintings hidden away in need of restoration. But then, you wouldn't want me to get my hands on them, would you? Even the prospect of putting me to work in a dank cellar couldn't induce you to trust me that far. I might make off with them, or do something equally dreadful to your treasures.'

Daniel eyed her thoughtfully. 'I doubt that,' he said, pushing the pen into a drawer. 'You might be an opportunist, but you aren't a fool. You wouldn't risk putting that slender neck on the block. Besides,' his glance was shrewd, 'you appreciate art work too well to deliberately spoil anything.'

He got to his feet decisively, curving a hand around her arm and bundling her towards the door. 'Come with me.'

'What—where are you taking me?' she muttered breathlessly as he marched her along the corridor. She had trouble keeping up with his long, swift stride.

'To the dank cellar, of course. Where else?'

They passed along several more corridors and down a flight of stairs before they finally arrived at a solid wooden door and he pushed it open, giving her a gentle shove into the room.

Laura stared around. There were windows on two sides, and it was furnished simply with a couple of comfortable chairs, and a very large table. It looked very much like a workroom, with several cloth-covered objects arranged around it.

'No bars at the windows?' she queried lightly. 'You must be slipping.'

Daniel's eyes glinted. Crossing the room, he removed one of the covers, to reveal an ageing canvas, and Laura moved forward to take a closer look. Fine cracks marred the artist's work.

'What do you think?' Daniel asked.

'It could be repaired,' she said. 'It wouldn't be too difficult.'

'There are a few others you could take a look at, as well.' He whipped the remaining drapes off the paintings and waited while she studied them.

'Well, what do you say? Will you do it?'

She regarded him quizzically. 'I'm not sure that I follow. I was joking, I didn't for one minute expect you to take me seriously.'

'You prefer to wait around for James?'

She gave him a twisted smile. 'There's a lot of work here. It might keep me at Oakleigh for weeks. Are you quite sure that you want to take that risk? Perhaps you should think it over for a while.'

'I don't need to. I'll pay you the going rate plus twenty per cent. What do you think?'

She considered the offer. If nothing else, it meant that she would have time to look for her own painting, and perhaps work towards getting it back. 'A short time ago,' she pointed out drily, 'you'd have done anything to keep me away.'

His glance skimmed over her. 'This way I get to keep tabs on you.'

She bit her lip. 'It wouldn't occur to you that you were mistaken in your opinion of me, would it?' she said, her voice low.

'No. My faculties are quite intact,' he said brusquely.

She gave him a look of glacial dislike. 'You're an insulting swine,' she said.

'But you'll do it all the same?'

'Why should I turn away work? I'm only here for the money, according to you, so I may as well live up to your expectations.' Serve him right that he'd offered her an extra twenty per cent. Her glance swept the room. 'I'll make a start tomorrow.'

*   *   *

Renovating paintings had a decidedly tightening effect on the neck muscles, Laura concluded with a rueful grimace, a few days later. She dropped a used cotton wool ball into a basin and rubbed a hand over her nape. Once she had started on this work, she had become swiftly engrossed, working through the day while James pored over the plans for the new leisure complex. It was worth it, though, she thought, casting a critical eye over the piece she was working on. Even in this short time, she had made steady inroads on the various pieces Daniel had selected, and she couldn't help feeling pleased with what she had achieved so far.

She put aside the painting she had been working on. She had done all she could on it for the time being, and she could do with a change. Perhaps she could sort out the new frame for the seascape that Daniel had mentioned the other day? It should be in his study.

Daniel was not in there, but she went in through the open door and took a look around. Although he used it as an office, it was a pleasant room, with plush red velvet curtains at the windows, and a rich, thick-piled carpet on the floor, dappled with evening sunlight. Apart from the usual clutter on the large desk, there was a filing-cabinet standing in a corner. There were books, too, one wall almost wholly taken up with them, and from what she had learned in running the shop she could tell that many of them were leather-bound first editions. A couple of easy chairs stood to one side, and over on the opposite wall was a door which, when she tried it, revealed a walk-in cupboard.

Laura sifted quickly through the assortment of boxes on the shelves and came to the conclusion that the frame she was looking for was not in there. She turned to go, and her hand snagged something and sent it tumbling to the floor with a dull thud. Picking it up, she saw that it was a book, a diary, but a quick inspection showed her that it had not suffered in any way.

'Have you found what you were looking for, or were you just browsing?'

The gritty sarcasm in the deep voice cut in on her thoughts, making her jump. She had not heard Daniel come into the room. 'Oh—I didn't—I thought—uh. . .' She trailed off, flushing under the cool cynicism of his grey eyes.

Her fingers fumbled, losing their grip on the richly embossed leather as she tried to put the book back on the shelf. Daniel caught it, his fingers tangling with her own, and she snatched her hand away quickly.

He said smoothly, 'I'll look after this, shall I?' weighing the book in his hand and replacing it on the ledge.

'I—I was looking for the frame you mentioned the other day—I——'

'You were sidetracked?' he finished for her,

lifting a dark brow. 'That doesn't look much like a frame to me.'

'Are you accusing me of something?' she snapped, her temper rising at his caustic remarks. 'What do you think I'm doing—looking for the low-down on your private life, your movements for the next month or so? You should have given me more time, I haven't managed to check up on all the details yet.' She glared at him, her cheeks heated. 'I suppose I could always sell my story to the Sunday papers—intimate revelations of my stay at Oakleigh—that would go down well, wouldn't it? Except that I don't have anything sensational to report, do I?'

Daniel's mouth made a bitter smile. 'It wouldn't be the first time someone has tried to manufacture a story from nothing.'

'And you have to tar everyone with the same brush? You know something? I feel sorry for you. You got your fingers burned badly and now you can't trust anyone, can you?'

Daniel's shoulders lifted carelessly. His glance moved around the room, taking in the paperwork on his table, the open drawer of the cabinet, then swerved back to her with deadly intent. 'It's a tough, competitive world out there, and the weak go to the wall. I'm not about to lose out on the chance of a major deal because I fell for the lure of a pair of hauntingly green eyes and a beautiful, cheating mouth. I want this contract, make no mistake. I'm taking no chances.'

He walked over to the desk and gathered up a file, locking it away in the cabinet with a slam. She drew in a fierce, shaky breath. It was worse than she had thought. It seemed that he believed her capable of any treachery.

'No,' she said carefully, 'you wouldn't, because making money is what makes you tick. Business deals get your steel trap of a mind working and nothing else matters, does it?' She swallowed painfully. 'People aren't important to you. They only get in the way—like my father. He had something you wanted, and you were prepared to see him destroyed to get it.'

'You don't know what you're saying,' he said roughly. 'Besides, it's human nature to go after what we want. You're no different. You just have more determination than most, and fewer scruples.'

Her fingers clenched at the jibe. He was referring to James, of course. He was so convinced that he was right about her. He would never listen to her side of things, but she tried, all the same. 'You're wrong about me,' she muttered. 'You have been all along.'

Daniel eyed her thoughtfully. 'I doubt it,' he said. 'You came to Oakleigh with a definite purpose in mind—James made that clear enough. You never intended to leave here empty-handed.

Perhaps you didn't get as far with James as you had hoped—that's why you jumped at the chance to stay on, even though it was snatching at crumbs. There had to be something in it for you.'

She took a deep breath and said, with a lift to her chin, 'You're right, there is something that I want; but not from James, from you.'

He waited, irony darkening his eyes.

She ignored it and went on, 'My painting. I want to buy it back.'

He gave a short, harsh laugh. 'What's this? Another whim?'

The bitterness in his tone puzzled Laura, and she looked at him questioningly, a frown etched into her brow. His mouth twisted at her expression, and she was aware of an unhappy sinking sensation in the pit of her stomach.

'Don't play the innocent with me,' he grated. 'You're as capricious as a butterfly trying out its new wings.' He studied her curiously, his eyes narrowing on her face. 'What makes you think I'd be prepared to sell it?'

'Why shouldn't you?' she said quietly. 'You have so many others that surely this one won't make all that much difference? I haven't even seen it on display, so it can't mean a lot to you.'

'Are you sure about that? Didn't you once say that acquisition was everything to me? Why should I part with it now, because it suits you at this particular time to have it back?'

His voice had a cold, cutting edge to it that made her pale rapidly, a sick feeling invading her body. She had expected him to give her some hassle over the painting, but she had nurtured some vague hope that after all this time he might be more prepared to view her request in a reasonable light, especially since she had been working for him.

Her tongue flicked lightly over her lips to moisten them. 'I've wanted to have it back for a long time now. I'm prepared to pay whatever you ask.'

He consulted the slim gold watch on his wrist. 'I'm afraid I don't have time to discuss the matter with you at the moment. I have to call my office in London.'

He moved to his desk, about to lift the receiver, when Laura said desperately, 'Daniel, I need to see it again—couldn't you. . .?'

'Unfortunately, I have to disappoint you.' He did not look as if it bothered him at all, and Laura felt her anxiety increasing. He said coldly, 'The painting is not in the house. Now if you'll excuse me, this is an important call and I prefer to make it in private.'

Laura stared at him, open-mouthed, her mind numbed by what he had said. He had bought it because he had wanted to hurt her, and for no other reason. He had not even kept it for himself, even though he had professed to admire it. It had all been an exercise in revenge. The room appeared to sway a little as she started towards the door, and she put out a shaky hand to steady herself on the jamb. He had sold her painting; the thought went through her head like a dirge.

'Shut the door as you go,' Daniel said, and she stayed quite still for a moment before she gathered up the shreds of her dignity and walked out.

James met her in the corridor. 'So there you are,' he said with a touch of impatience. 'I've been looking everywhere for you. I might have known you'd be with Daniel.'

Coming on the heels of her set-to with his brother, Laura stiffened at the terse note in his voice. 'Is something wrong?' she asked wearily. 'I was looking for a picture frame in Daniel's study so that I can make a start on another piece of work.' She did not need to explain her actions to James, but the last thing she needed now was to argue with him as well.

'It's time you took a break,' James muttered, studying her with a frown. 'You've been working too hard. It isn't good for you to push yourself like that. You're already looking pale and washed-out.'

Laura smiled weakly. 'Thanks,' she said with a rueful curve to her mouth. 'That does a lot for my self esteem.'

His expression was sheepish. 'Nothing a night out won't cure. Why don't we drive out somewhere and have a meal? I know a nice place where

the food's out of this world, and we can dance,
too. What do you say?'

Laura thought about the work waiting to be
finished. Maybe she had been pushing herself. She
had not wanted to give Daniel any chance to find
fault, nor had she wanted him to accuse her of
taking a long time over the work in order to
prolong her stay. Her mouth tightened. They were
both clamped in a bitter feud that could only end
in misery, but it would not be she who paid the
price, Laura determined. Daniel was beleaguered
by devils of his own making, and she would not
let them bring her down, too. She said, 'You're
probably right. I could do with getting out for a
while. Just give me time to shower and change,
will you?'

Sifting through the contents of her wardrobe,
she picked out a plain white sheath dress, its only
adornment a thin, gold-coloured belt. She was not
sure where James had it in mind to take her, but
the classic simplicity of the dress made it one that
would be suitable whatever the occasion. She
decided to leave her hair down, contenting herself
with running a brush through its shining length,
then she put the finishing touches to her lipstick,
and added a spray of perfume.

Daniel was crossing the hall as she went down
the stairs, and for a moment her step faltered. He
stopped suddenly, and she tensed as she felt the
icy rake of his grey glance shifting over her slim

figure. His slow, head-to-toe appraisal of her made her cheeks burn and she began to wish that she had chosen a different dress, one that did not mould itself to her curves in quite the way that this one did.

Her pride reasserted itself. Why should she let him intimidate her like this? She continued down the stairs, her head high, a blaze of defiance in the look she slanted his way.

'Going somewhere?' he enquired silkily.

'That's right,' she answered in a low voice. 'James is taking me out for a meal.' She lifted a brow. 'Any objections?'

His mouth curled in contempt. 'James never really stood a chance, did he? Not once you had made up your mind to get that ring on your finger.' He paused. 'You reckoned without me, though, and that was a mistake. Your biggest mistake, because you don't dazzle me, not by a long way, and I'm the one who'll deal with you in the end.'

'Oh? What did you have in mind?'

His shook his head. His voice was frighteningly soft, the voice of a predator about to devour its victim. 'You wouldn't like to know, Laura. Believe me.' A muscle jerked spasmodically in his jaw. She watched it, then lifted her gaze, and shock washed over her skin in an icy ripple as she encountered the glitter of anger leaping in his dark eyes.

'I like James,' she said unsteadily. 'No matter what you might believe.' She turned and walked away from him, but not before she had seen the answering derision edge his mouth.

James took her to a newly opened nightclub a few miles out of town. It was all chrome and smoked glass, flashing lights, and disco music in the intervals when the three-piece band took a break. She studied the menu, while James ordered drinks—an iced martini and lemon for her, lager for himself.

'What will you have to eat?' he asked.

'Steak, I think—medium, and a salad.'

James handed the menu back to the waitress who appeared at their table. 'Make that two, will you? And we'll have a bottle of the red.'

Laura sat back in her seat and tried to relax. The throb of disco music beat in her head, and her fingers tapped out the rhythm absently on the arm of her chair. She had to strain to hear James when he spoke.

'I was beginning to think we'd never get the chance to be alone,' he said. 'I've hardly seen anything of you these last few weeks. Just when the work on the new development was coming to a close, and I thought we'd have some time to be together, Daniel found you a stack of work to do.' He took a long swallow of his drink. 'I'm beginning to think he had it planned all along.'

Laura registered the complaint in his tone, and

said lightly, 'I expect the project was top priority with him. He wanted to get on with it as quickly as possible.'

'He could have done that in London,' James pointed out with asperity.

Inwardly, Laura agreed with James, but she wasn't about to tell him that. She had no intention of fanning the flames of disagreement between the brothers. She murmured, 'He obviously thought that working with you was beneficial. If anything, it shows that he has faith in your abilities, doesn't it?'

James was in no mood to be mollified. 'The push with that is over now,' he said flatly. 'All he has to do is submit the plans to the company and wait for results. So why is he still at Oakleigh?' He clamped his lips together while the waitress set down the food in front of them.

'Maybe he's taking a break,' Laura suggested, helping herself to salad. James was in a fractious mood, and she could have done without that today, after her disagreement with Daniel. Already she was feeling the beginnings of a headache, and the persistent thrum of music in the background was no longer a pleasant distraction.

'He could do that anywhere in the world,' James muttered disagreeably. 'No. There's only one reason why he's staying on at Oakleigh. He wants to be near to you. He thinks he can make some headway with you if he stays around.' He glowered into his drink, then finished it off rapidly.

She stared at him, nonplussed, then gave a short laugh. 'That's ridiculous.'

'Is it?' His jaw tightened. 'Then why is he thinking of sending me away?'

Laura was startled. 'I didn't know that—he must have given you some idea of his reasoning, surely?'

James signalled the waiter and ordered more wine. 'For you too?' he asked, but she shook her head.

'Fruit juice, thanks.' She rubbed abstractedly at the ache in her temples. 'What did he say about your going?'

'Something about new developments abroad. He said I ought to broaden my perspective—what he really means is, he wants me out of the way to leave the field clear for himself.' His lip thrust out moodily.

'You are a fool, James,' she said, torn between wry amusement and exasperation. Sometimes he reminded her of a small boy. 'How can you seriously have worked that one out? The whole idea is absurd.' Why on earth couldn't he see that for himself?

James scowled and stabbed at his french fries with his fork. 'I'm not so sure about that,' he muttered.

Laura ran her finger around the cold rim of her

glass, studying him through her lashes. 'Let's not allow Daniel to spoil our evening,' she murmured coaxingly.

'He'll do whatever he can to come between us,' James persisted. 'I've seen the way he watches you. He's waiting, brooding.'

She pushed her glass away. 'Not in the way that you think,' she said heavily. 'He doesn't even like me, James.'

'You're wrong. You two had something going for you a long way back, and you may have thought it was dead and gone, but he's out to revive it.'

The colour ebbed from her face.

James said huskily, 'I knew about it, Laura. I've always known, but I believed it was over. When I invited you to stay at Oakleigh, I knew you weren't in love with me, but I hoped that we might get closer as the weeks went by.' His voice dropped. 'I hadn't bargained for Daniel, though. He was the real fly in the ointment. Even telling him about the planned engagement didn't put him off.'

Laura watched worriedly as James started on another drink. Trying to keep her voice steady, she said, 'There may have been a time, millions of years ago, when he liked me a little, but his real interest was always my father's property. I was only secondary to that, or even a means of getting it.'

She toyed with her salad, moving it around her plate negligently with her fork. 'I've made an enemy of Daniel, but you mustn't let that come between you. He only means to protect you.' She suppressed a sigh. 'You should tell him that we aren't involved, you know, James. Because we aren't, and we won't be. Not in the way that you want. I like you, you're my best friend, but I never meant to give you the impression that there could be anything more. I'm sorry.'

James's features set in a tormented line. 'What did I do wrong? What do I have to do to make you love me?'

Laura gazed at him, stricken. 'Nothing,' she whispered. She let her hands fall to her lap, curling her fingers into a tight little ball. 'I'm sorry. I do want us to be friends, James.' She swallowed. Her throat felt tight, painfully dry. 'I don't want to make trouble between you and Daniel. I would never have agreed to visit if I had realised what was going to happen.'

'It isn't your fault,' he said slowly, his voice faintly slurred. 'But you had better take care, Laura. I know my half-brother better than you do, it seems. He's after something, and he always gets what he wants.'

He stood up abruptly, swaying a little. 'We'll go on somewhere else. Dance the night away. This place is beginning to be a drag.'

He fumbled for his car keys, and Laura said

worriedly, 'I don't think. . .' but he was already walking away, stumbling a little between the tables, and Laura got to her feet quickly, wondering how she could stop him. He had been drinking steadily since they arrived at the place—he was in no condition to drive.

She settled the bill, then followed him out into the foyer. 'James,' she said, 'I——'

'If you don't want to come, I'll go on my own,' he said, waving the keys.

She hurried forward. Someone caught hold of her arm, taking her by surprise. She recognised him from the university. Kevin something, she remembered.

'Do you need some help?' he asked, and she nodded unhappily.

'He's had too much to drink—he shouldn't drive. . .'

'I know—James never could hold his liquor.' He paused. 'I was at a table near you—I didn't mean to pry, but I gathered something was wrong. I wonder if perhaps he could do with some male company right now, a friendly ear?'

'I—I suppose so.'

'Why don't you leave him to me? I'll take him on somewhere and put him in a better frame of mind. You don't need to worry about him, I'll see that he gets home OK.'

Relieved, she said, 'Thank you, you're being very thoughtful.'

'That's what friends are for,' Kevin said. 'Will you be all right if we leave you? Do you want me to call a taxi for you?'

Laura saw James beginning to weave his way along the pavement outside. 'I'll be OK,' she said. 'You see to James.'

She watched as Kevin retrieved the keys from James and helped him into the passenger seat of his car. After a minute or two they pulled slowly away from the kerb, and she followed their progress until they were out of sight.

She had not wanted to hurt James, but what could she have done? He wanted what was not in her to give, not to any man. Perhaps by nature she was cold, and that was something she had to come to terms with, because no one had ever come near to stirring her senses except. . . She closed her mind on the thought. Daniel was the last man on earth she should have any feelings for. Her heart was locked away, clamped in a vault of stone.

The discovery that the public telephone at the club was out of order when she went to call for a taxi was what she had come to expect from a day in which everything had gone wrong from start to finish. Gritting her teeth, she walked out into the street, and prayed that the phone booth on the corner had not been vandalised. The click of her stilettos rang out in the quiet night, an eerie sound that made her glance around to confirm that she

really was alone. Usually there were one or two
people about, either going into the club or coming
out.

A man stepped out of the shadows, approaching
her, and she jumped.

'On your own, darling?' he called. 'Boyfriend
let you down, has he? Let me keep you company.'

Laura said sharply, 'Go away,' and put on a
spurt to the telephone. She heard him coming
after her, and twisted round, ricking her ankle. 'If
you follow me,' she gritted, 'I'll scream and bring
everyone out of the club on to the street.' She
glared at him, her breathing fierce, her mouth
tightly echoing the warning that her green eyes
were flashing.

He put up his hands in mock surrender, and
began to back off, slowly. Laura kept her gaze on
him as she stepped into the booth. She dialled
quickly, rubbing her sore ankle against her other
leg while the call went through. She would wait
for her taxi in the safety of the club.

A young couple had emerged from the
entrance, and Laura gave a sigh of relief, using
them as cover while she hurried back into the
foyer. All she had to do now was hope the
wretched taxi didn't break down on the way to
Oakleigh.

A light was on in the main living-room when
she returned to the house, and that surprised her,
because it was very late and she had expected—

hoped—that Daniel would either be out, or in bed. He was neither.

He appeared in the hall as she came in quietly, intent on making her way upstairs without being noticed. She wasn't up to a confrontation with Daniel right now. Her ankle was throbbing, as well as her head, and she didn't need any more problems tonight.

'What happened to the car? I hardly expected you to come back in a taxi.' He was holding the stem of a brandy glass between his fingers, rolling the amber liquid around its bowl with a gentle, hypnotic motion, and she stared at it, her attention fixed anywhere but on Daniel.

'Nothing happened,' she muttered. 'Just a change of plan.'

His grey eyes narrowed on her face. 'Where is James?'

'He—he went on somewhere,' she said in a low voice and moved towards the stairs.

'Without taking you with him?' His glance slid over her slender shape, and a flare of heat coursed through her limbs at the insult implied in that slow deliberation. 'Why should he do that?'

'Ask him yourself,' she retorted, incensed by the way his eyes were still moving over her, touching the tawny brilliance of her hair, shifting to caress the rounded swell of her breast, the curve of her hip, gliding over the smooth length of her legs.

Daniel lounged against the newel-post, watching her with lazy speculation, his eyes half closed, deceptively somnolent. She returned his gaze uneasily. If she had learned anything, it was that he was always at his most dangerous when he had that smoky, slumbrous look about him.

'I shall,' he promised. 'Poor Laura. You don't look as if you enjoyed yourself very much. Why is that, I wonder? Food not up to much? Or was the music too loud?' He swirled the brandy in the glass, savouring the bouquet appreciatively. 'I don't suppose it was either of those things.' He put the glass down on a low table by the stairs. His cool assurance was aggravating, jarring her already stretched nerves.

She said flatly, 'I've a headache. I decided to come back here and take some aspirin.'

'Something must have happened,' he continued to probe maddeningly. 'What was it? An almighty row? Did James cotton on to the game you're playing?' The soft malice in his voice made Laura shiver, a tremor of ice crawling along her skin.

She said, 'I'm going up to bed,' but he blocked her way, his face darkly cynical.

'What went wrong, Laura?'

'That's my business,' she snapped. 'If you'll excuse me——'

'I don't think so.' He made no effort to move, standing in front of her at the foot of the stairs, every inch of his powerful frame a threat. She regarded him in stony silence, her chin jutting angrily.

'Where is he, Laura?' he questioned her remorselessly. 'Why isn't your lover with you now, soothing that beautiful brow?'

The mockery glinting in his dark eyes was too much after the strain of the last few hours. She knew a sudden, urgent desire to slap the taunting smile from his face and be done with him for ever.

'I'm sick of your disparaging remarks,' she said fiercely. 'I've had enough, do you hear me? He isn't my lover. I don't have a lo——' She clamped her mouth shut, regretting her outburst instantly. Damn him for making her lose her cool. Damn him. With a violent swing at his chest she tried to push her way past him, only to have him jerk her back to him, forcing her to look up into the glitter of those steel-grey eyes.

'Is that so?' he muttered harshly. 'How revealing.'

Her teeth bit into the soft inner flesh of her lip. Why had she let him bait her that way?

His mouth made a grim smile. 'You're still playing it cool, aren't you? Making him wait for it, keeping him on edge; you'll torment him, tantalise him—you're good at that, aren't you, Laura?'

'You're vile. I hate you,' she flung at him. 'I don't think of James in those cold-blooded terms. I'm not—I don't have to explain myself to you,' she stormed. 'Let go of me. I'm going to my room.'

'You're running away,' he said with cool derision. 'You can't bring yourself to tell me what went wrong between you tonight.'

Rage shot through her like a spark igniting petrol. 'You want to know what happened—I'll tell you. I told him I wanted his money, and a stake in Oakleigh. You took my father's business and now I want something in return.' Her voice cracked, and she tried to twist away from him. Her ankle wrenched with the movement and she gave a gasp of pain, bending with it, tears of frustration springing to her eyes. 'Let me go, damn you.'

Daniel swore under his breath and swung her up into his arms, marching with her towards the living-room. He ignored her shrieks of protest, depositing her roughly on the sofa.

'You've no right,' she fumed, doing futile battle against the crushing strength of his grip on her wrists. 'You can't do as you please, just because you're stronger than me. You think you can get away with anything—well, you——'

'Shut up, Laura.' His tough, lean body was a hair's breadth from her, stifling her with its hard, forceful masculinity. She struggled, her breath rasping. He moved back a little. 'And sit still.' He slid his hand over her leg, moving it down across the bruised, tender area of her ankle. 'How did you do this?'

'Never you mind. I don't need you to act as nursemaid, or to enquire into my private life. What I do has nothing to do with you.'

'It has everything to do with me,' he said with cool arrogance. 'You had an escort when you left here; you came home alone, late at night. When you are a guest in my house, your safety has to be my concern, whether you like it or not. Now, I'm asking you for the last time—why didn't James bring you home?'

'I told you. He went on somewhere else with a friend. I didn't want to go with them. I had a headache, which is getting rapidly worse, thanks to you.' She snapped her mouth shut stubbornly, her eyes sparking dangerously.

'He was drunk,' Daniel said curtly.

'I didn't say that.'

'No. You said a lot of other things and it's perhaps just as well. It's about time they were given a proper airing.' He eyed her coldly. 'Since when was I responsible for taking your father's business? I seem to recall it was a legitimate deal, contracted between us.'

'On paper, perhaps. You hounded him, and you didn't give up, even after he died, and for what? You haven't touched the property since you took it over.'

'Your vision of the situation is distorted, as

usual,' he said, his tone clipped. 'Obviously your father did not want to confide in you, for reasons of his own. Perhaps because you would have been ideally suited for what I had in mind, and that would have brought more pressure to bear on him.'

Her lashes flickered. 'What are you talking about?'

'I wanted to set up a gallery. A small, select place, where new artists would get a chance to exhibit.' His mouth made a grimace. 'Your father didn't like the idea when I put it to him. He turned down the opportunity point-blank, even though both you and he would have had a big stake in it. He preferred to waste all his time and energy on keeping the premises as a shop. I wanted to help him, but he was too blind to see it.'

Laura was stunned, her attention riveted on his taut profile. Somehow, instinctively, she felt he was telling the truth. His bitterness was too real. 'I didn't know,' she whispered. 'I had no idea.'

'Would it have made any difference? You were so convinced that I was the villain of the piece, about to grind your father into the earth, that whatever I said would have been suspect.' His voice was whiplash tight, and she flinched visibly, her troubled eyes scanning his features restlessly. Was he right? Had she let her father's rancour cloud her mind? Daniel had bought her painting, knowing how much she treasured it, and that was hardest of all to forgive, but perhaps that was only a measure of the hurt that he had felt at their combined mistrust.

'I—I don't know what to say,' she stammered. 'I made a mistake, I misjudged you. I thought. . .' She shook her head, the silken mass of her hair drifting across her cheeks, hiding her bewilderment. 'My father was a difficult person to know. He kept everything to himself—perhaps he bottled things up too much, after my mother died, I don't know. But he was full of doubt and suspicion, and I believed him—I can't make amends for that, I don't know how.'

She looked up at him in confusion, and Daniel reached for her, tilting her face towards him, his fingers strong and lean on her jaw. He studied her intently, his gaze moving over every feature with slow, intimate purpose.

'Perhaps there is a way, after all,' he muttered.

She was very still, as his fingers moved over the smoothness of her skin, tracing the curve of her cheek, the soft, full line of her mouth. Her lips trembled under his touch, and he kissed her then, tasting her with a slow, sweet thoroughness that left her senses reeling, her fingers curling into the hard wall of his chest. He moved closer, sliding down beside her, his warm breath drifting lightly over her hair as his arms encompassed her.

It was like finding a haven, a refuge from the

storm, and it seemed the most natural place to be right then. He claimed her mouth once more, teasing her with tantalising butterfly kisses, easing her back into the soft cushions.

'You taste of honey,' he murmured, 'sweet and inviting—delectable.' A low whimper escaped her as his lips feathered along the slender, vulnerable column of her throat, pausing to nuzzle there. His fingers shifted, spanning her waist, and moving slowly upwards to linger with heat-induced vibrancy beneath the soft fullness of her breast. It was the lightest, gentlest touch, and yet it made the blood race through her veins in a hot tide, leaving her weak and shaken.

The light, sweeping caress of his hands made her skin tingle with feverish sensation, and she twisted restlessly under the gentle expertise of his fingers. She had not even realised that he had dealt with her zip until the soft fabric of her dress slithered down over her shoulders. She muttered a protest, but he bent his head towards her, and his lips trailed hotly over her skin, searching out the smooth valley between her breasts. She gasped, and tried to move away, to escape the heated promise in his gleaming gaze, but he would not let her go, pinning her wrists with his hands when she would have broken free.

'Don't try to hide from me, Laura,' he muttered, 'you're so lovely. You're all that I imagined.'

Flame sparked in his dark eyes, searing her as he swept aside the flimsy lace of her bra, and gave his attention to the softly rounded contours of her breasts. A faint smile touched his mouth, a curving, sensual smile of lazy anticipation, and then she felt the light brush of his lips sweeping over the warm silk of her skin, and a wild, fierce shiver of delight coursed through her body.

He teased her with the slow nuzzling of his mouth over each smooth crescent, until the nub of her breasts firmed in aching, exquisite torment. She cried out as his tongue found each hard little peak in turn and curled around it, stroking languidly, pleasuring her until her need was urgent, frantic, and she found her body lifting, pressing closer in shameless response to the teasing, provoking ministrations of his lips. She mumbled incoherently, caught in a whirlwind of desire, a storm of sensation that tossed her mindlessly into delirium.

'What is it you want, my sweet?' he said huskily. 'Tell me. Do you want me, is that it?'

She had always wanted him. In her heart, in her mind, in every part of her being. She knew that now. Was this love, this bewildering, painful emotion that was besieging her? No matter what had happened in the past, she could not escape the fact that her life had been an empty shell without him.

He kissed each quivering bud in turn, while his

hands stroked deliciously over the smooth plane of her abdomen, feathering down over her thighs. His lips followed, 'Yes,' she whispered, 'oh, yes. Daniel, please, I. . .'

He shifted slightly, looking down at her, and said softly, 'And what of James? Isn't he the one you love? The man you're going to marry?'

She stared at him in blank confusion. His body was taut, held in check, his mouth a hard line.

'Had you forgotten about my brother?'

'No, I——'

'You don't love him,' he persisted harshly. 'I've known all along that you were only using him——'

'No—it was never like that—we were just friends——'

'Not true, Laura,' he broke in sharply. 'James is head over heels about you, but we both know that doesn't cut both ways. It was only ever the money that was of any importance to you.'

Laura was stunned by the change in him. 'That isn't true!' she gasped.

He smiled, a sardonic travesty of a smile, and let his gaze slide over her. She tried to writhe away from the burning whip of those grey eyes flicking mercilessly along the length of her body, but he held her still.

'It doesn't matter,' he said roughly. 'There's no reason why we can't come to some arrangement over this. It doesn't have to end here.' His hand wandered over her fevered skin, moulding her soft curves. Her heart hammered wildly, banging against her ribcage until she thought she would faint if its pounding did not stop. 'I want you, Laura,' he said huskily. 'You've always known that. It's a hunger in me that goes on and on; you've got me raging like a furnace for you. You're beautiful, sensual, you make me ache to have you to myself.'

Panic rose in her chest like a smothering blanket as he bent towards her. 'No,' she mouthed in hoarse protest as his lips brushed like the sweep of silk over her bare breast. A sob broke in her throat. 'No,' she cried again, and his head lifted.

'Think of it as a business agreement, a contract, if you like. That way, we both get what we want.'

Her brittle control shattered, her breath coming in harsh gasps. She cried raggedly, 'No—no. . . I wouldn't have you. . .if you were the last man on earth.'

CHAPTER SIX

LAURA spent a sleepless, wretched night. When the first weak rays of sunlight at last began to filter through the curtains she dragged herself from her bed and went to shower, hoping that the pulsing jet of water falling on her aching body might help to revive her enough to face the day ahead.

Misery curled in her stomach like a tight knot. How could things have gone so terribly, painfully wrong? After she had at last admitted to herself that she loved Daniel, had never in the depths of her subconscious stopped loving him, her worst nightmare had become reality. The humiliation he had wreaked on her could not have been more bitter. His cruel treatment left her racked by a growing sickness for which there was no cure. At the least she had hoped that he might come to care for her a little, but that had been just a crazy dream, doomed from the start, and last night he had crushed it completely and finally with his callous actions. He hated her, a small cold voice whispered inside her head, and now the hurt would go on and on without an end.

The shaming truth was that in his embrace she had let her love for him come to the surface, and he had ruthlessly, with brutal deliberation, thrown it back in her face.

'I want you,' he had said, but only as a whore was what he had meant. His cynicism was such that he could coax her to the heights of sensual pleasure and still keep that quintessential part of himself coldly impassive. A shudder went through her body. She could not stay here any longer and suffer the insult that he was inflicting on her. She would go as soon as she could get her things together.

The smell of coffee drew her to the breakfast-room some time later. James turned from his seat by the window to look at her as she walked in, and she felt a sharp sense of remorse when she saw the dark shadows lurking in his eyes.

'How is your head this morning?' she asked quietly, pulling out a chair to sit beside him.

He grimaced. 'I think I must have gone ten rounds with a cast-iron bell last night. My ears are still ringing.'

'That bad, huh?' She gave him a sympathetic smile. 'Kevin must have taken you on somewhere, I gather. You were pretty late getting in.'

His brows pulled together. 'To tell you the truth, I don't remember much about what happened after I left you. I know I talked a lot of rubbish about making a fresh start, and trail blazing, and so on, and then the conversation got around to what we were both going to do with ourselves now that university is behind us. Kevin said something about working in his father's business. None of it's really very clear, though.' He frowned. 'I was an idiot last night. I just hope I didn't do anything too stupid—make more of a fool of myself than I had already with you.'

'You didn't,' she said quickly. 'It was my fault, I hadn't realised——'

He shook his head. 'I should have had more sense. You told me from the outset, but I had to keep on trying. I made a mess of things all round.'

'No. Forget it, James, it's in the past now.' She stared blankly ahead. A lot of things were past, finished. Perhaps in years to come, when she looked back to this episode in her life, the pain would have dulled to a nagging ache. It was all she could hope for.

'I'm sorry about leaving you the way I did,' James muttered.

'I was OK. Don't worry about it.'

He reached for her hand, saying anxiously, 'We are still friends, aren't we? I haven't ruined that?'

'Of course.' She gave his fingers a gentle squeeze in return.

'Then—don't take what I'm going to say the wrong way, I'm not asking with an ulterior motive in mind—but—when I go to Europe, why don't you come with me? There's nothing to keep you here, is there?'

'I——' Laura stiffened, her answer frozen on

her lips, as the door swung open, and Daniel walked into the room, his stare narrowing on their clasped hands.

James shifted uncomfortably and slowly withdrew his fingers while Laura stared ahead, her face devoid of colour, her back rigid. She would not acknowledge Daniel's presence by so much as a gesture, or even the flicker of an eyelid.

He came over to the table and poured himself a coffee, taking his cup over to the opposite window where he stood, looking out in silence. His profile might have been carved from stone.

James gave his attention to Laura once more. 'What do you say, Laura. Will you come with me?'

'I don't think so.' Her voice was strained, a reaction to Daniel's brooding presence. 'Anyway, it isn't practicable——'

'Why not?' James interrupted with soft urgency. 'I can't see any problems.'

'I can't leave for Europe just like that,' she said quietly. 'There's the flat, and Maggie, and all the loose ends that have to be tied up. I've contracts lined up for the next few months.'

'Excuses,' James said shortly. 'You can just as well freelance over there as here.'

Daniel moved slowly and Laura caught the edge of his warning glance. He was not saying a word but he was telling her that she would rue the consequences if she went away with his brother.

What would he do? she wondered. Would he tell James how he had brought her to the brink of mindless passion and then dealt her the killing blow?

She drew her coffee-cup towards her, tracing an invisible line along the handle. 'It isn't that easy,' she said.

'Of course it is,' James pushed her objections aside. 'There's nothing that couldn't be dealt with if you really wanted to come with me. You could be ready to leave in a matter of hours. We could go and get your air ticket this afternoon.'

'No,' she answered, 'but I am leaving here. As you said, there's nothing to keep me here, now. I'm going back to the flat.'

'You can't,' James said, shocked.

'I've made up my mind,' Laura told him quietly, picking up her cup and sipping carefully.

Daniel spoke for the first time. 'Running away, Laura? Why is that?'

She ignored his silky toned question, but her green eyes were hard as she stared at him over the rim of her cup.

He said unpleasantly, 'I hope you haven't forgotten your commitments here.'

By a supreme effort of will, she managed to keep her voice steady. She said frigidly, 'Commitments can be broken.'

His mouth tightened. 'But not these ones. You have work to finish.'

James's glance flicked from one to the other, the veiled hostility in the air bringing a jagged crease to his brow. He said into the chill silence that had descended, 'Well—I have some things I need to sort out. I'd better get on with it. Laura— I'll talk to you later, OK?'

She gave him a brief nod, her lips fastened against the tide of anger that threatened to escape.

Daniel put down his cup, and walked with James to the door, saying coolly, 'I'd like a word with you in the office, James.' Reaching the door, he turned, resting one palm flat against the jamb, his gaze sweeping Laura. 'I have to go to London for a few days. I shall expect you to remain at Oakleigh until the work is completed. By my reckoning, that means you will still be here when I get back.'

'And if I choose not to stay in this house, what then?'

'I'm paying you well for this commission, had you forgotten?'

'Not at all,' she said, injecting ice into her tone. 'Please keep your money. I shall be leaving.'

'Think hard about the consequences of that, Laura.' He threw her a grim smile. 'I have a great many contacts in the art world. I could easily see to it that you find it increasingly hard to get work.'

'That's blackmail,' she protested angrily.

'A nasty word,' he said coldly. 'I prefer to think of it as insurance.'

He left the room, and Laura glared at his departing figure in impotent fury. He had trapped her, knowing perfectly well that she would not risk her career by opposing him. She had no option but to follow the dictates of his devious mind. Her fingers clenched. Why was he doing this to her? Surely he couldn't want her here, any more than she wanted to stay? It was only that he meant her to suffer, so that he could savour his revenge.

She heard his car start up within the hour, the revving of the engine sounding brisk and impatient, but it was only when the screech of tyres had faded into the distance that she breathed a shaky sigh of relief. She went straight to the workroom. If she had to stay here until the renovations were complete, she would waste no time. With luck, if she worked day and night, she might be finished and away before he returned

Heather brought her lunch on a tray and Laura took the opportunity to ask about the picture-frame that she needed and had not been able to find.

'I'm sure Daniel ordered one,' Heather said, 'but it doesn't appear to have arrived yet. It shouldn't be more than a couple of days, I imagine. If it hasn't been delivered by Thursday, I'll give the company a ring and chase it up.'

'Thanks,' Laura murmured, hoping that it was on its way, 'I'd appreciate that.'

James found her concentrating on a particularly tricky piece of canvas when he came into the workroom next day. Setting aside her brushes and bottles, she leaned back in her chair, running a tired hand through her hair.

'How goes it?' he enquired, and she shrugged lightly.

'Not bad, I suppose.'

He said cautiously, 'I'm sorry if I caused friction between you and Daniel yesterday. You obviously had some disagreement going, and I barged in and made matters worse.'

'It wasn't important,' Laura muttered stiffly. 'Anyway, he's gone now, so it's all water under the bridge.'

'He'll be back. In double-quick time, if I know Daniel. He won't want to let you slip through his fingers. He's afraid you might take off with me.' He paused, sliding a finger over the polished surface of the table. 'I never did stand a chance with Daniel waiting in the wings.'

Laura sighed. 'Forget him. You're looking for reasons, but he doesn't have anything to do with you and me.'

'Even if you didn't love Daniel, you wouldn't be interested in me, is that it?' He gave a rueful smile.

Laura's harsh intake of breath was audible. She said faintly, 'What makes you think——'

'You're not the first one to fall, you know, not by a long way.'

She felt all the colour drain from her face. James went on in a matter-of-fact tone, 'Women do go for Daniel. It isn't just his wealth, but he can't see that, of course. He's too cynical for his own good.'

Dismayed, she realised that none of her protestations had any effect on James. He saw too clearly what she had tried to keep hidden. Perhaps that was why he had pursued her all this time, she saw with sudden clarity. Had the seed of jealousy been planted in his mind long ago, even before she had met him? Was James in constant rivalry with his brother?

He said quietly, 'I accept that you've made up your mind about not coming to Europe with me, but will you come and see me off at the airport?'

'Of course. When do you have to leave?'

'It's an early morning flight, so I thought rather than travel overnight I'd catch a train to London tomorrow and book into a hotel. I've a few things to see to there before I go.'

Laura nodded. 'I suppose I could do some shopping while you sort yourself out.' It meant some time out of her schedule at Oakleigh, but she felt she owed James this, at least.

'That's settled then,' James said. 'I'd better leave word with Heather where we'll be staying, in case anything urgent crops up. I seem to remember Kevin saying that he was going to give me a ring about something.'

He booked them into a large modern hotel, which was only a short drive from the airport. Their rooms were next to each other on the third floor, both spacious and well furnished, with views over a green expanse of beautifully set-out gardens.

The view made little impression on Laura, though. Over the last few days her mind had shut off from all but the effort of getting through the long hours as best she could.

While James made last-minute visits to the bank and various other premises, she wandered around the shops, not really seeing what was on display. Her gaze flicked desultorily over the latest fashions and accessories, without any particular interest. Only an art shop, selling canvases and oils, caught her attention briefly.

She wondered what had become of her painting. Daniel's decision to sell it had been proof of his indifference at the time—but since he had learned of her involvement with James things had changed. He meant to hurt her, punish her in some way if he could. So what chance was there now that he would give her the name of the buyer? The one precious link she had had with her past had slithered out of reach.

She had dinner with James that evening in the hotel restaurant, which was quietly elegant, with subdued lighting and tables set apart by discreet screens. Plants trailed their glossy green foliage over the trellis-work, and soft-hued flower arrangements contrasted with crisp white linen cloths.

Picking over the cool, delicious melon starter, she said, 'Daniel seemed pleased with your ideas for the leisure complex. Did he include many of them in the final plans?'

'Two or three in the end, I think,' James answered. 'He needed to make sure they were feasible and compatible with what he wanted to achieve, before he altered any of his designs to suit. The major part of the work was his own, but he did seem pretty taken with some of the constructional aspects I pointed out. Part of the course that Kev and I did in the last year included a study of new materials and some of their advantages in building work, and, though Daniel already knew about them, he wanted to chew the fat a bit.' James took a careful sip of his wine. He was being sparing with his drink this evening, Laura noted. He was keeping himself very cool and clear-headed.

'He's always been one to keep abreast of the latest technology,' he went on. 'He believes in innovation, provided that it's solidly based. It used to scare me, the way he was so much on the ball—I was afraid to put a foot wrong, but I needn't have worried. He doesn't suffer fools gladly, but he's always ready to listen, and absorb other points of view, even if he doesn't act on them.'

Laura smoothed an invisible crease from the skirt of her dress, hiding a frown. She had never found Daniel ready to hear what she had to say. Perhaps he had a blind spot where she was concerned.

James fingered his napkin while the waiter served the main course. They had both opted for salmon, accompanied by a creamy hollandaise sauce.

She said, 'He obviously appreciates that you have something to offer, now that your time at university is over.'

'I'm not sure about that,' James said, with a wry smile. 'I've a feeling my education is just about to begin, with this trip to Europe as the starting-point.' He forked the tender, moist fish. 'He thinks a year or two travelling the world looking at different styles and techniques will broaden my outlook. Perhaps I misjudged him before; he seems to be thinking of drawing me fully into the business eventually.'

Laura arched a delicate brow. 'Then this is a celebration meal. We should have ordered champagne.'

James grinned. 'There's a bottle on ice in my room. We could polish it off after we've eaten.'

She regarded him thoughtfully from under her

lashes, and he said quietly, 'I'm not thinking of enacting a seduction scene, I promise. I didn't ask you here for that reason. Just a farewell meal, because I don't suppose I'll be back for several months.'

'In that case, I'll accept,' she murmured. 'But one glass, mind, or I shall be floating all night.' To bring the conversation back to a more level footing, she said, 'Do you think Daniel will get the contract?'

'I'm not sure what competition he's up against, but I shouldn't think there will be anyone to beat him. He's good. He knows his job and he puts his own inimitable stamp on everything he's involved in.'

'When will he know?'

'Within a few days, I should imagine. He's in London now to submit his plans. After that it's just a question of waiting to hear.'

They ate a fruit dessert, and finished the meal with liqueur coffees. As Laura savoured the cognac in hers, James retrieved a piece of paper and a pen from his jacket pocket.

'This is the address where I'll be staying for a few weeks,' he told her. 'Write to me, won't you, and let me know how things are with you.'

She took the paper and put it in her bag. 'I will,' she said, adding, 'Make sure you do the same.'

James gave her a smile. 'Thanks for coming

with me, Laura. Now,' he pushed his liqueur glass to one side, 'shall we go and sample that champagne?'

He led the way along the carpeted foyer towards the lift, and Laura caught sight of their reflections as they passed a mirrored wall. James wore a smart, dark suit, teamed with a crisp, pale blue shirt and darker blue tie. Her dress was a halter style, smoothly fitting in the bodice, and low cut in the back, with a skirt that swished lightly as she walked. She had pinned her hair up for this evening, and she was surprised to see how cool and sophisticated she looked. Her image did not reflect the way she felt, the wine and liqueurs and good food had combined to make her head pleasantly muzzy.

James opened the door to his room and ushered her in. 'I'll find a couple of glasses,' he murmured, and she sat down on the bed, letting her glance stray to his suitcases, still open on the floor.

'Have you sorted all your packing ready for your flight?' she asked, dubiously observing the bags and various packages that were lying around.

'There are just one or two last-minute things to put in,' he said. 'I bought a few bits and pieces today—a shirt and a couple of pairs of trousers.'

'Can I help?' she asked. He came back with the glasses and popped the cork of the champagne.

'You could put them in for me while I change into something more casual for the journey,' he said, pouring the drinks. He took off his jacket and threw it down on the bed, then loosened his tie. Picking up a pair of denims and a sweater, he started towards the bathroom.

She called after him, 'What about your passport and ticket, are they in your flight-bag?'

'You sound like my mother,' he said with a grin in his voice, before he closed the bathroom door.

Laura started to pick up the things he had bought that day. He had scattered most of his belongings about the room, and she retrieved his new trousers from a chair, folding them carefully.

An imperious rapping on the door interrupted her thoughts and she paused, her brows pulling together. Who could it be at this hour? It must be one of the hotel staff—but they hadn't ordered room service. The banging became louder, more insistent; whoever it was didn't intend to go unnoticed. Dropping the trousers into the case, she went to the door.

'I might have guessed,' Daniel said tightly. 'You just couldn't bear to leave him, could you?' The anger in him was frightening to see, the sharp steel of his eyes menacing her. She almost reeled from the savagery of his expression, but then he had pushed past her into the room, and her fingers fumbled on the door, pushing it shut. Shaken, she watched the grim set of his mouth as his glance homed in with unswerving accuracy on the champagne resting in its bucket of ice on the table.

'How romantic,' he sneered, lifting out the bottle.

She said, 'What are you doing here, Daniel?'

His glittering gaze shot fiercely over her, taking in the shining upward sweep of her hair which left vulnerable the naked line of her throat and shoulders, moving along the smooth, sensual drift of her dress, down to her feet, attractively encased in high-heeled shoes.

His stare shifted back up over her body and heat raced through her limbs as if he were touching her with his hands. She tensed, colour flowing along her cheekbones.

'Have I disturbed your cosy little love-nest?' he said, his mouth curling. 'What was this, some kind of celebration?' He rammed the bottle back into its bed of ice and glowered at her.

'Of a kind, yes,' she admitted, trying to ignore the intimidation evident in his hard-boned frame.

'I don't need to ask what it is you're so ecstatic about,' he grated. 'Where is he?'

Her mouth firmed. 'If you mean James, he's in the bathroom.'

He narrowed his eyes to dark slits. 'What are you playing at, Laura? You're supposed to be at Oakleigh. Have you lost all interest in a career? Do you imagine James will support you?'

Laura lifted her chin, attempting a cool defiance. She would not let his threatening manner throw her off balance. Daniel did not like to be thwarted. He wanted his own way, and he was used to getting it, but now it was time he learned that he could not browbeat everyone.

'Since when were my movements any concern of yours?' she enquired with a haughty lift to her brows. 'I had not realised I was accountable to you.'

'Don't be facetious,' he snarled. 'I rang the house to find out the time of James's flight and Heather told me that you were both away. I couldn't believe you'd be so stupid.'

'That's hardly my problem.' She began to move away from him and his hands shot out, gripping her fast.

'You're not going with him,' he said tersely. 'I won't allow it, Laura.'

She glared at him. 'You aren't in a position to dictate what I do,' she countered, breathing hard. 'If I made up my mind, you couldn't stop me.' She had no intention of going with James, but she would not tell him that. He was not going to dominate her.

He dragged her towards him. 'Why are you doing this?' he muttered harshly. 'You don't love him——'

She said hoarsely, 'What do you know of my feelings? When have you ever listened?'

'I know how you are when you're with me,' he said roughly. 'I know the way your body responds—you can't hide that, can you?'

She took a long, shuddery breath. He enjoyed tormenting her. He wanted her to squirm—it gave him a warped sense of satisfaction to make the hot shame course through her body. She shut her eyes as if that would make him disappear and the ache he stirred in her would somehow fade into the background.

'You're not for him,' Daniel breathed, and something in his voice made her tremble. She looked at him, and was shocked by the taut, hard-boned rigidity of his face. His jaw was clenched, and his eyes had darkened to a violent slate-grey.

'You're hurting me,' she muttered, and for a moment his grip tightened.

He said thickly, 'Sometimes I want to hurt you. You bring out the worst in me.' He pushed her away, and she rubbed at the reddening bands where his fingers had marked her tender skin. He was angry, because he wanted her away from James and she was defying him. He wanted her away from his family. That was what concerned him most of all, that was the message that he was trying to enforce.

'Shouldn't you let your brother run his own life?' she asked shakily.

Daniel's teeth came together, his words forced through them. 'I'd knock him out rather than let him go off with you.'

Laura stared at him, distressed, the pulse in her throat thudding erratically. When she spoke, her voice was strained with the tension that his hatred wrought in her. 'I doubt it will come to that. Talk to him; maybe that way you'll find out what James wants.'

Suddenly, she was very tired; all her energy had drained from her. Slowly she walked to the door, and went out into the corridor, shutting behind her all the pain and misery.

If only it were that simple. Why was she condemned to love a man who could see no good in her? Back in her own room, she sat down on her bed, and struggled with the bewildering welter of emotions that besieged her. How could she ever come to terms with what she felt for Daniel? He might have been blind, from the way he had ignored any attempt she had made to explain her actions in the past, and now she was too weary to make the effort. It was no use. The sooner she finished her work at Oakleigh and cut any connection between them, the better.

Looking into the mirror on her dressing-table, she saw that her face had lost all vestige of colour. She was wiped out. There was nothing left. She picked up a comb, and began to tidy up the loose tendrils of hair that had escaped from the pins that held it in place. She wished that she could smooth out the ache in her heart as easily, but the pain stayed with her, there was no balm to take that away.

She heard the light tapping on her door, but

ignored it. It was not time yet for James to leave the hotel for the airport, and she did not want to face anyone until then. Whoever it was would soon give up and go away.

'Laura.' It was Daniel's voice, but she did not answer. 'Let me in, Laura. I know you're in there.'

How could he know? she thought dully, and realised that the light must show under her door.

He knocked again, insistently this time, and she said quietly, 'Go away.'

'I want to talk to you.' When she continued to ignore him, he started to hammer violently on the door, and she began to worry that the people in the rooms about them might complain.

'I don't have anything to say to you,' she muttered. 'Go and bother someone else.'

The pounding on the door became so intense that her hand went to her throat in panic. She went to open the door. He looked as if he was about to batter it down with his shoulder. He saw her and straightened. 'If you don't stop harassing me,' she said sharply, 'I'll call the management and have you evicted.'

'I owe you an apology,' he said, stepping inside the room, and she stared at him blankly. 'I came to say that I'm sorry.'

She blinked, her eyelashes flickering across her cheeks. He closed the door and leaned against it, staring at her.

'You were right,' he said quietly. 'I didn't listen. I was too obsessed by what I thought I saw, to take your feelings into account.'

Recovering slowly, she said, 'Presumably you've spoken to James.'

He had the grace to look chastened. 'He told me you were going to see him off at the airport. I should have given you the chance to explain.'

'It might have been better if you had not jumped to conclusions in the first place,' she retorted bitterly.

'I realise that,' he said. 'When I heard you were with him, it was like a red mist rising in front of my eyes. I wanted to do murder.'

She said stiffly, 'Am I supposed to be grateful that you don't give in to these impulses? I'm afraid I'm not.'

'I was wrong,' he muttered. 'Do you want me down on my knees begging forgiveness?'

'That won't be necessary,' she grimaced. 'If you've said what you came to say, perhaps you would go now.'

Daniel's glance slanted over her. 'I said I would drive James to the airport. He'd like you to come along.'

Her expression was carefully blank, veiling her thoughts. Glancing at the watch on her wrist, she said, 'In that case, I'll get my jacket.'

* * *

After they had seen James on his way, Daniel took Laura back with him to Oakleigh. There was little traffic on the roads at this early hour of the morning, and London was soon left far behind. The drive was a relatively silent one, with Daniel preoccupied, and Laura mulling resentfully over the events of the day.

His apology had done nothing to soothe her ragged nerves. As far as he was concerned, he had made a mistake in this instance, but that did not mean that he had changed his basic opinion of her. Most likely he believed that his threats had made her think twice about doing anything foolish where James was concerned. She twisted her fingers together in her lap, studying them abstractedly. The sooner her work was completed, the better.

They arrived at the house at around breakfast-time, and Heather came out to greet them.

'Did James go off all right?' she asked. Laura did her best to answer the myriad of questions she asked while Daniel garaged the car. 'You look a bit peaky,' Heather commented, casting a concerned eye over her. 'Perhaps some food and a hot drink will perk you up a bit. A parcel has come from the gallery, by the way—the frame Daniel ordered. I put it on the table in the study. You could look it over later, when you're rested.'

'Thanks, I'll do that,' Laura said.

In fact, it was late afternoon when she finally

came around to seeking it out. She had spent some time finishing off work that she had begun on one of the larger canvases, but, once that was out of the way, she was able to turn her attention to framing the smaller picture. Daniel was not in the house. He had been engaged most of the day with the workmen on the estate, something to do with outbuildings that were being erected, and that gave her a small measure of relief. She could not cope with his nearness. Her feelings were still too raw.

As soon as she went into the study, she saw the large brown paper parcel on the desk. It had been opened, but Heather had folded the wrapping over again, to protect the edges. Carefully, Laura drew the packaging to one side to reveal the ornately carved frame. Lifting it out, she could see straight away that it was exactly right for the picture.

There was something else hidden in the folds of paper and cardboard, though, and she put the frame to one side, curiosity compelling her to investigate.

Later, she might have wished she had left well alone, taken the frame and gone back to the workroom, but she had not done that; she had seen the painting lying on the pristine bed of polystyrene and known it for what it was with a flash of horrified recognition.

The pain her chest was like a knife-thrust. She

almost cried out. Trembling, she reached for the painting. It was a harbour scene, sunlight glinting on the water, brightening the sails of the colourful boats.

She passed her fingertips lightly over the surface of the picture, and the tears burned at the back of her eyelids. For so long, she had waited for this moment, and now that it was here there was only pain.

Daniel had lied to her when he said he did not have her mother's painting, and the lie was like a burn searing through her body.

CHAPTER SEVEN

'HEATHER said I'd find you in here.'

Daniel's voice sounded far away, muffled by the roar of blood that was drumming in Laura's ears. The shock of discovery left her mind numb with misery, clouded in a blanket of despair.

She stared down at the picture in her hands. Slowly, with infinite care, she placed it on the desk-top. She had waited for years to retrieve it, yet now any joy she might have felt had been destroyed, completely and utterly.

Daniel came towards her. 'Did you find the frame? I haven't had a chance to look at it yet.' He slid his arm lightly around her shoulders and her body recoiled, jerking like a doll on a string.

He eased back, shooting her a long, hard stare. 'What's wrong, Laura? Are you ill? Can I help?'

She struggled to find her voice. 'I think—you've done enough,' she managed unsteadily.

'I don't understand.' He frowned, searching her pale face intently. 'What's the matter? Tell me.'

'You won't have seen this,' she said dully. 'Take a look, and tell me that I'm not really seeing it.' She held out the painting, conscious that her fingers were trembling and she was unable to control them. 'You lied to me,' she said hoarsely. 'Why did you lie to me?' Her fingers traced a delicate pattern over the gilt frame. 'You knew how much this meant to me, yet you said you didn't have it. Why did you do it?'

Daniel took the picture from her, studying it thoughtfully, his brows drawn together. 'I didn't lie,' he said, lifting his gaze to her.

She gasped, a sharp, painful intake of breath. 'You said——'

'I said it was not in the house.' He put the painting down on the table. 'In fact, I had sent it away for reframing, something I had been meaning to do for a long time. There was a piece chipped from one corner.'

'You deliberately kept the truth from me. That's the same as lying,' she said in a choked voice.

'Not quite. You annoyed me with your pretence that it meant so much to you. I decided to let you stew for a while.' He shrugged. 'I put all thought of it aside after that—I had to wait until it came back with the new frame.'

Laura sent him a hostile look. 'What do you mean—pretence? You knew very well I never wanted to part with it in the first place.'

'What game are you playing now, Laura?' Daniel's mouth crooked scornfully. 'The painting that was supposed to be so precious to you was sold to me for a very high price, much more than its real worth. You were happy enough to take the money then—why quibble over it now? You don't have to try to redeem the past. I know all there is to know about you, and I've learned to accept it. We don't need to argue over this.'

Stung by his cool arrogance, she said tightly, 'If you didn't want to argue about it, why did you hold on to it for all this time, except to get back at me? You don't want it, you never did. You're hard and unfeeling. I might have expected that any dealings with you would be cold and calculating.'

'Is that right?' he said bitterly. 'That's how you think of me? That makes us an evenly matched pair, doesn't it? Why don't we do business?'

In one swift move he compelled her towards him, his palm flat on the small of his back, his other hand cupping her chin, forcing it up so that she was imprisoned by his strong, unrelenting fingers. 'You say you want the painting. I want you. Just how desperate are you to have this picture, Laura?'

With a sob breaking in her throat, Laura wrenched herself away from his cruel grip. 'I told you, once before,' she said raggedly, 'I wouldn't have you at any price. The sooner I'm finished and out of this house the better as far as I'm concerned. I hate you, Daniel Warwick, and all you stand for.'

She ran out of the study, and fled up the stairs

to the sanctuary of her own room, locking the door. He did not come after her, and she lay on her bed fighting the tumult of her emotions until the dark shadows of evening crept about her and she at last fell into an exhausted sleep.

Laura did not see him for two days after that. He was called away to one of his developments in the south-east, and he was supposed to be going on from there to London. She used the time to make headway on the last of the canvases that had to be restored.

Her head ached from the unhappy thoughts that churned around inside it, a sick tension clamping her like a tight band. He had treated her with a cool insolence that was unforgivable, as if he had been the injured party and not herself. She could not understand his harsh attitude. He had been bitter and sceptical about her feelings, almost as though he believed she had been the one to instigate the selling of the picture.

Why should he be so convinced that she was mercenary in all her dealings with him? There was no reason—unless—— The thought exploded on her with the suddenness of a storm—had her father told Daniel that she was the one who wanted the picture sold? That might account for Daniel's continuing disbelief.

She was in the workroom when he came back, and it was clear immediately that he was in a foul temper. He jerked the door open and strode in, his eyes raking over her figure with undisguised contempt. She swallowed nervously. She had seen him angry before, but never like this; he was white around the mouth, his eyes dark with fury as he stared at her.

'So you're still here,' he ground out savagely.

She jumped at his tone, and said, defensively, 'I haven't quite finished yet. I'm working as fast as I can—it shouldn't take much longer.'

'That isn't what I meant,' he bit out. 'You know it. The same way you know why I'm back here right at this moment.'

Laura chewed at her lip. 'Has something happened?' She tried to think of any problems that might have come up in the last few days, and drew a blank. Then she said tentatively, 'It's nothing to do with the leisure complex, is it?'

He smiled viciously. 'You see, what did I tell you? I knew you would come up with the right answer. It didn't take long either, did it? I expect you also know how a rival company submitted plans that were almost identical to mine, in use of materials, design, etcetera, etcetera. The only major difference, of course, was in cost estimates. But you'd know that, wouldn't you, Laura? They would have to be lower than mine, wouldn't they? Not too much, just enough to ensure the contract.'

She heard him with dawning horror. What he was saying was unthinkable. Someone had managed to get hold of his ideas in detail, and had used them without compunction. But how? His work was all carried out at Oakleigh, so who could—she snapped off the thought, her mouth trembling with dismay.

'Why did you do it, Laura?'

Her head lifted at the unaccustomed pain she heard in his voice. 'I didn't do anything,' she told him unhappily, bewilderment clouding her eyes. All that work had come to nothing. No wonder he was so angry.

'Don't play the innocent—that butter-wouldn't-melt-in-your-mouth routine, spare me that, at least.' His fingers bit into her arms. 'You don't need that ploy any more.'

There was a rage in him that would not be sated. She saw it, and paled. He looked as if he could crush her with his bare hands, and still go on hurting her. She tried to push away from him, then, afraid of the raw violence that snapped in his eyes, but she couldn't win, she was powerless against the strength in those cruel hands.

'Was it because I sent James away, is that why you did it? Or was it because of that damn painting? Tell me why, Laura?' He was shaking her, so hard her teeth rattled.

'It wasn't me,' she said breathlessly. 'You have to believe me.'

'Who else could it have been? It had to be you. No one else had the opportunity, or the reason. You said yourself that you hated me.'

She gulped for air. 'Stop—shaking me,' she said, her head snapping back helplessly. 'I can't—breathe.'

He stopped, but his fingers stole around her throat. 'I'd like to kill you,' he growled. 'I'd like to squeeze the breath out of you.' She knew real fear then—her green eyes were wide with terror and her lips moved, but no sound would come out. She stared at him like a hunted animal at the mercy of its most deadly enemy.

A muscle in his cheek began to jerk erratically, but his jaw was rigid, clenched against the flood-burst of his anger. For a moment, he held her, his eyes flaming with unholy light.

'What have you done to me?' he said hoarsely. 'What have you turned me into?'

His grip slackened, and she gave a shuddery, rasping sigh as relief hit her. Faintness made her sway a little, and his arm shot out to haul her on her feet. She was too weak and dizzy to fight. She wanted to move back, away from him, but the wall nudged the back of her legs, and he was too close, his body a hard, potentially lethal weapon. She moistened her parched lips with the tip of her tongue.

'You're driving me out of my mind,' he said roughly. 'I'm going crazy for a woman who doesn't give a damn about me. Isn't that a laugh? Why aren't you laughing?'

She said in a voice barely above a whisper, 'You

never believe a word I say. You're so full of suspicion. How can I fight that?'

His face was chiselled in hard, gaunt lines. 'How can I be anything else but suspicious? Since the day we met, you've wound me up, had me in knots. I need you, and I can't get rid of that need. It's burning inside me, destroying me; no matter what you've done, I want you. That never changes. It goes on and on, tearing at me. It doesn't matter what you are, I've got to have you, Laura.'

His hand clamped her head, his fingers lost in the silky mass of hair at her nape as his mouth came down on hers with bruising force. It was a punishing kiss, full of the pent-up tide of his emotions, meant to dominate and bring her into line. She resisted, stubbornly closing her mouth against the onslaught, but he would not be deterred. With firm insistence he probed her lips with his tongue, until he had gained the entry he wanted, and a groan of satisfaction rumbled in his throat. He plundered the soft, moist interior without hindrance, tasting, savouring with complete disregard for her choked protest. That invasion made her weak. She was dazed by it, but she would not give in. Her fingers beat against his chest, but his arms closed tightly on her.

His head lifted and she stared into his face, reading the determination there. There was a dark flush along his cheekbones, and his eyes were half closed, brilliant, a fever burning in them that brought a piercing shaft of panic to clench her stomach. His hands shaped her, drawing her against his body, and he kissed her again, heated possession in that kiss. He was seeking a response, demanding it, and she tried desperately to ignore the beguiling quiver of sensation which was slowly uncurling deep inside her.

His hand shifted, grazing her breast, his mouth travelling across her cheek, her throat, coming to rest against her hair. She pushed at him with the flat of her hands, but he forced her back against the wall and she heard the rip of her blouse as she tried to twist away. His eyes moved over her, she felt them burning on her skin, and then his hand was dragging the material aside, stroking, ravaging her senses with its smooth, silky caress. Excitement spiralled in her; she felt the hardening thrust of her breast against his palm and despaired. Her body twisted, arched, her head moved restlessly from side to side as the fire in her veins built up under the glide of his hands. Hands that were unsteady, she realised with a sense of shock; he was trembling with heat and desire, and the knowledge of that unnerved her.

Her struggles became desperate, but the heated pressure of his lean thighs held her still. Her skirt was caught and she could not tug it free. She felt the thudding of his heart against her ribs—it was beating crazily, wild and out of control. His breathing was harsh, rapid, feathering over her throat. His fingers trailed downwards over her thigh, lingering as he encountered the bare skin above her stockings. He muttered something against her hair—husky, unintelligible words, then his fingers moved on, exploring, stroking with increasing intimacy. Fierce tremors shook her as he enticed her along a path of exquisite discovery, and she cried out, trying to deny the heavy ache of her body even while she was yielding to the urgency of that sensual assault.

Her legs were weak, she was falling, slipping, her body arching; she was sick with shame. Daniel's mouth brushed the soft skin of her neck, made a swift foray to nibble lightly at her earlobe.

His gaze ran over her, heavy-lidded, smoky. 'What power do you have over me, Laura?' he muttered thickly. 'I'm hooked on you. You're in my bloodstream like a drug, I can't get enough of you.'

She gave a soft moan, her head falling against his shoulder as shudders rippled through her body. He was speaking of passion and need, but love didn't come into it. She loved him and she needed to be loved in return. Anything less was a mockery.

She spreadeagled her fingers on his chest, finding a desperate strength to push him away, and he stared at her, dazed.

'Nothing has changed,' she whispered, but she was saying it to herself. 'It will never be different from this, will it? It's a sickness, you're the sickness, a kind of fever that I can't shake off.' She looked up at him, her mouth trembling, her eyes bright with unshed tears. 'You want me, but that's all it is. A craving that has to be satisfied at all costs. My feelings don't matter to you. You've been warped by the past. Whatever happened to you made you bitter, and now you can't trust anyone.'

She took a deep, shaky breath. 'I didn't take your plans and give them to a rival company. I don't know who could have—but of course you would never believe what I say.' She started to move away and he reached for her but she slapped his arms away with a violence that shook them both. 'Don't touch me,' she said fiercely. 'Leave me alone.'

The tears dammed up behind her eyelids, but she would not let them fall. There was no hope, no future for them together. Nothing could be based on mistrust, and she knew she could not live with suspicion constantly festering between them.

Daniel was staring at her, as if he was seeing a stranger. He made no further move towards her as she went to the door—and it was just as well, because right at that moment she would have picked up anything that came to hand and fought him off with it.

'I'm leaving here,' she said. 'I should never have come in the first place. I've had enough of the Warwicks—of you. I don't want your money, I don't want anything to do with you. We've no link in this world, we're separate entities, galaxies apart. But I always knew that.'

The phone shrilled, a discordant sound in the quiet of the room, setting Laura's teeth on edge. She opened the door, and Daniel said, 'You can't go, Laura—we have to talk.'

'I don't think so. I've said all that I have to say. Shouldn't you answer that phone?'

'Never mind the phone. You can't leave her yet——'

'No,' she agreed softly. 'I still have work to finish, don't I?'

He seemed to hesitate, and she left the room, closing the door quietly behind her. She heard him pick up the receiver, cutting off the shrill sound that jarred the air.

Would he carry out his threat to cut her off from her contacts in the art world? It was a risk she had to take, because if she stayed here any longer she would go to pieces, her self-control would fragment. All she wanted was to be alone, to come to terms with the grief and heartache that threatened to tear her apart.

* * *

She heard him leave the house half an hour later.

'There was an accident on one of the sites,' Heather told her. 'One of the workmen has been taken to hospital with a suspected leg fracture. Daniel's gone over there. He said to tell you he should be back tomorrow morning.'

'Thanks, Heather.'

It was all Laura needed to know. An opportunity to leave quietly and without fuss. She rang for a taxi, then packed her cases, throwing her belongings into them in haphazard fashion. She would be long gone before he came back. There was no point in prolonging the agony. It only meant more heartbreak, and she could not take much more of that. Clicking the locks firmly home, she took the cases downstairs and waited for the car to arrive.

She had decided that she would not go back to the flat, for a while at any rate. Maggie would understand if she told her she needed some time to herself. She would make a clean break of it, that was the only solution. There would be a small cottage, perhaps, along the coast, where she could find some peace, and try to rebuild her shattered life.

It was only when she was safely installed in the back of the cab, and she turned her head to see Oakleigh receding into the distance, that the slow, salt tears escaped and trickled down her cheek.

CHAPTER EIGHT

LAURA studied the canvas in front of her with a critical eye. It had been a particularly difficult piece to work on, demanding all her concentration, but that was exactly what she needed right now. Something to fill the aching void that had grown in her since she had left Oakleigh.

She rubbed the base of her spine where the little knot of tension had spread into a dull ache. Maybe it was time to take a break, go for a walk along the sea-shore to blow the cobwebs away. This one section had caused her more than its fair share of problems, including a stiff back.

Stretching her limbs wearily, she acknowledged that she had been pushing herself to the limit, working through the day and long into the evenings in an effort to bury her troubled thoughts under the weight of activity, but it was not having the desired effect. Her mind still wandered with unshakeable determination to Daniel. Even when she dropped into an exhausted sleep there was no respite. He was woven into the fabric of her dreams, tormenting her with dark, elusive images throughout the night. This morning had been no different. She had woken feeling drained.

She could not go on like this much longer. Daniel was not part of her life any more and she had to come to terms with that. The decision to go had been a tortured one, but it had been the only way open to her if she was to keep her sanity. Daniel had always been full of doubt and suspicion towards her, and she could not live under that dark cloud any longer. Loving him made it too painful.

Pushing her fingers through the red-gold mass of her hair, she stood up and went over the sideboard, staring pensively at the pages of James's letter, lying in creamy contrast against the polished wood. She picked it up and quickly scanned the lines. James was her one tenuous link with Daniel, and there were times when she caught herself searching his letters desperately for a hint as to what his brother might be doing now, what plans he had, and then she had to pull herself up sharp, because that was dangerous ground.

She turned away abruptly, biting her lip, and reached for her jacket from its peg on the back of the door. A walk would do her good, she decided, stuffing the letter into her pocket. There were plenty of tracks to follow in this quiet, wildly beautiful part of the coast. It was one of the things that had helped make up her mind to rent this small cottage for the rest of the summer.

Listening to the undiluted savagery of the waves

crashing on to the shore brought an answering echo in the painful shattering of her heart. She had believed that here she might begin to sort out the tangled web of her emotions, and emerge, if not whole—because that was never going to be possible—at least pieced together enough to face up to the rest of her life. So far she had not succeeded too well. She had concentrated her energies on finishing off work she was already contracted for, but she ought to be thinking ahead. Perhaps she ought to take up the lead that James had offered in his letter. At least that would get her out and about, give her a new challenge to meet.

'Since you're continuing with the free-lance work,' he had written, 'you might be interested in talking to a friend of mine. New contacts are always useful, after all. If you give his secretary a call, I'm sure she would be happy to arrange a meeting.'

Laura pulled the letter out of her pocket and stared thoughtfully at the phone number scrawled on the notepaper. It was worth a try; James was right, the more contacts she had, the better, especially if Daniel should prove difficult and try to curtail her career as he had threatened.

In the end, the arrangements were made so smoothly that it was less than a week before Laura found herself on the way to the address the secretary had given her.

She drove several miles on the coast road, then turned inland for the last portion of the journey. Checking her directions several times, she eventually approached a select group of residential properties secluded from general view by a protective screen of mature trees.

Parking the car by an elegant brick-fronted tenement, Laura stepped out on to the pavement, scanning carefully for the flat she wanted. A highly polished brass nameplate informed her that it was on the second floor, and she took the stairs quickly, emerging into a wide, carpeted corridor. Her heels sank into the soft pile. Flat 2a had its own small vestibule and she paused a moment to straighten the kick pleats on her slim-fitting skirt before knocking.

The door opened, and her shocked eyes encountered the man who stood there, her lips parting on a gasp of pure dismay.

'I hope you had a comfortable journey?' The hard line of Daniel's mouth belied the polite consideration of his words.

She turned swiftly, and started to walk away, confusion and anger welling up in her like a fountain, but he had caught her before she had gone two paces, reeling her in like a hooked fish that had unwisely taken the bait. She glared at him, her face pink with outrage.

'What are you playing at, Daniel?' she demanded hoarsely. There was bound to be some cold-blooded reasoning behind his actions, and she simply could not, and would not, go through that torment again. She tugged in vain at her arm, locked in the vice-like grip of his hand. 'Did it bother you so much that I left your work unfinished? Is that what this is about? Well, I'm sorry, but you're wasting your time. I'm not going back to Oakleigh.'

'That's what I thought you might say,' he said with a tight grimace. 'Which is precisely why I'm here.'

Through the hard knot in her throat she said, 'You'd do better to turn around and go home right now. It won't make any difference. You're going to have to get someone else to tackle the last of the canvases.'

'We'll go inside, shall we?' he suggested smoothly, manoeuvring her with insulting ease towards the door. She dug in her heels, and felt a small spark of satisfaction when a muscle began to flick spasmodically in his jaw. 'I'm sure you would prefer our conversation to be continued in private,' he said tersely, his dark brow lifting.

'I prefer to leave,' she contradicted him. 'I've nothing at all to say to you.'

'You're mistaken,' he gritted softly, ignoring her choked outburst and levering her through the doorway. 'Besides, I have quite a lot to say to you. After all, you left so abruptly we didn't get to finish our discussion.'

'You mean, you didn't get the chance to insult me properly. What do you imagine I've done this time—made off with the family silver? That would be about the level you put me on, wouldn't it?'

He said coolly, 'Come into the lounge.' His hand at her back urged her into a large room, and her gaze snagged on the simple uncluttered lines, so different from Oakleigh. There was a chesterfield, a low, glass-topped table, a couple of armchairs, and a luxurious, cream-coloured rug contrasting with the deep russet of the carpet.

'Can I get you a drink?' Again there was that cool urbanity to his tone that grated on her nerves.

'No, thank you,' she answered stiffly. 'I don't need a drink.'

He walked over to a bar in a corner of the room, and helped himself to Scotch. 'You won't mind if I do?' he enquired, looking at her over the rim of his glass as he tilted it to his lips.

She turned away. Her eyes were stinging, and she did not want him to see the way he affected her. She did not want to see the cruel mockery of his expression.

Her legs, already threatened by an insidious weakness, brushed the chesterfield, and she sat down, straight-backed, her nerves on edge. It was a mistake, she found, because now, when he came to the table and straightened after placing his glass on the smooth surface, he towered above her, and her eyes warily registered her extreme disadvantage.

She tried to cover her anxiety in talk. 'Does this place belong to you?' she asked, and her voice sounded unusually strained, which was not surprising given the circumstances.

'I bought it some years ago,' he said dismissively, his brows making a sharp angle. 'We had established that you were staying at Oakleigh until the job was complete. Why the sudden departure? Don't you think we had things to talk over?'

Laura passed the tip of her tongue over her dry lips. How could she have stayed, loving him and having her feelings torn apart by his mistrust? If he had loved her—but he did not, and that was what had made it so hard to bear. It had all seemed so hopeless.

She attempted a shrug. 'What was the point in talking, if you were intent on disbelieving everything I said?'

'So you packed up and walked out, just like that? You must have known that sooner or later I would catch up with you.'

'Are you so determined on revenge? I left, and for once you didn't get your own way. Did that upset your tidy apple-cart?' Her mouth moved jerkily. 'What are you going to do about it, Daniel? Beat me, get it out of your system?' The taunt had a bitter edge.

'Don't think I'm not tempted,' he gritted

harshly. 'These past few weeks you've goaded me beyond endurance, flinging your affair with James in my face. How much do you think I could stand without going off my head?'

'You were afraid I'd get him, and milk the coffers dry, weren't you?' she said with a grim little smile. 'As if I were ever any threat to you.'

'I wasn't about to stand by and watch it happen. You aren't the one for James.'

'No——' Her throat closed. 'I'm not good enough to marry your brother, but an affair with you would be just fine, wouldn't it? Well, I don't see it that way.'

'You never did.' His eyes darkened to the colour of slate. 'It was always no go with me. Yet you wanted me down on my knees, and you waved James in front of me like a red rag.'

Laura's hand crept to her throat. 'That isn't true. It wasn't like that. Oh, perhaps it started out as a way of teaching you a lesson, but somehow it all got out of hand.'

His jaw clenched. 'You could say that. You had me out of my mind. When I thought you had gone to that hotel with him, I wanted to kill my own brother, and, more than that, I wanted to throttle the life out of you. I had never felt that way before, I'd never experienced anything like the surge of emotions I felt then.' He stared at her broodingly. 'I wouldn't ever have believed I could come to know what it means to be insane with jealousy.'

She said huskily, 'You know the truth about James and me. There was never an affair. We're friends, that's all.'

'Maybe. But when I saw you together it always looked more than that.'

'And you thought that gave you the right to treat me as a whore.' Her eyes glittered, smarting from the dammed-up tears which she would not acknowledge. Even now, the memory of his callous treatment of her brought with it a hot flood of shame.

'No.'

Her head came up at the harsh inflection in his voice, her eyes widening. He came and slid down beside her on the chesterfield. 'I never thought of you in that way, but I couldn't get rid of this driving need. It swamped me; it got in the way of everything. I couldn't stand your being with him. I only had to imagine you together and I was out of my mind. I want you, Laura, you know that. I want you for myself. That's why I tried to threaten you into staying at Oakleigh, and when that didn't succeed I had to find a way to get you here.'

His arms came around her, and Laura tried to ward him off, panic running through every nerve fibre. 'I'm not—available,' she said brokenly. Her chest felt tight, encased in a steel band. 'What do you expect of me, Daniel? Maybe you have been hurt in the past, and you've forgotten how to trust, but I'm not like that—I'm only human—I want warm, human emotions, all the normal kind of feelings that people have. But you feel nothing for me—you made that very clear, painfully clear. Under that cool, hard-bitten exterior of yours, there's just a cool, hard-bitten heart. You thought money was my sole motivation and you had no hesitation in throwing that back in my face. You wanted sex, that's all, and when you couldn't break me down, you tried to buy me.' Her voice broke on a sob and she averted her face quickly from his instant scrutiny.

'You make it sound so meditated,' Daniel murmured huskily. 'It wasn't like that, believe me. What I feel for you is not something I can come to terms with easily; it's primitive, Laura, violent, a hunger that won't be satisfied. I'd use any means I could to get you.'

'Even so far as overlooking my unsavoury mercenary streak?' She sniffed, rubbing at her eyes with the back of her hand. 'Isn't that taking things a bit far?'

His finger traced a line over her shoulder, smoothing the fine silk of her blouse. 'If it came to that, so be it.' He regarded her steadily; his eyes serious, a deep, fathomless grey. The fingers made light circles over the silk, sending spirals of heat to radiate across her skin. 'When your father offered the painting for sale, he told me that you wanted the best price you could get for it. At first I didn't believe he was serious, but then someone else put in a bid, and I had to step in, rather than see it disappear for good. I didn't know what was going on—you had seemed so genuine about the picture, and I thought perhaps it was all tied up with the sweet, innocent act—but whatever game you had been playing, I couldn't stand by and let a stranger have it. I decided that if it really mattered to you, you'd contact me.' A bleakness entered his eyes. 'But you didn't. There was no word, just four barren years, until you sold the shop, and decided you'd like the painting in return.'

Laura's breath caught painfully in her chest. 'I didn't want it sold. My father was desperate—he owed you money.'

'I wasn't pushing him for it. At the same time, I did what I could to get his suppliers to hold off with their demands for payment.'

Laura chewed at her lip. 'But he said—there was no other way——'

'I don't believe that was true. I think he wanted to be rid of it—perhaps it was too strong a reminder of the wife who had left him. She had put her love of painting before her feelings for him, and he could never forget that. He once said that you and your mother were very similar in looks; I don't suppose that made it any easier for him over the years. It might also have had something to do with putting him off the idea of a gallery.'

'He never talked about it. Perhaps he couldn't come to terms with it. I know that he would have liked to get away from the painting side of things, and veer more towards the antiques, but restoration was what he was skilled at and it was difficult for him to change course. As it was, he went under.'

'Your father was never much good at handling the money side of things. That's the reason he went downhill, Laura, not because of any pressure from me.'

She stared at him, her eyes dark, her teeth worrying at the soft inner flesh of her lip. He was asking her to accept that her father had deceived both of them.

'Don't you believe me?' His fingers tightened on her, drawing her towards him. 'Why should I lie? None of it matters now, anyway. Only this is important, you and me, here and now, everything else is past.' A spark flamed in his eyes, his gaze wandered over her, burning where it touched, lighting a fuse of awareness deep within her. Her heart began to thud wildly, hammering against her rib-cage.

His head lowered, his mouth only inches from her own, and she pulled away from him, panicking, hot with the knowledge that she had been close to succumbing to the seduction of his embrace.

'I won't—Daniel, it's all finished, there's nothing for us, don't you see that?'

His mouth firmed. 'I see it just beginning, Laura. You belong with me. You might try to deny it, but it's there all the time, that magnetic pull that draws us together. You can feel it, too, I know you can, so why won't you give us a chance?'

'It won't work,' she muttered shakily. 'How can it? How long will it take for the gloss to wear off—a month? Two? Then you'll start to remember how you lost the bid for the complex, and you'll know just where to lay the blame, won't you?'

'I didn't lose the bid. The contracts are being drawn up in London for me to sign.'

Her mouth dropped open, and he shut it gently with a finger beneath her chin. Taken completely by surprise, she let her gaze wander over his face in searching intensity, trying to see behind the glitter of his dark eyes to the mind beneath. It was an impossible task, and suddenly the warm, coaxing pressure of his lips stole all thought from her, closing on her own in a sensation of pleasure she had not prepared for. It took her by surprise, the sweet thrill of that kiss, the heat of it spreading through her veins like molten honey. Her eyelids flickered and closed as she absorbed the lazy sensuality of his mouth moving on hers. The effect was drugging, it took her senses away and left her floating on a soft cloud of candy-floss.

He growled softly, huskily in the back of his throat, and when she looked at him she saw the smoky brilliance of his eyes, the dark flush running along his cheekbones. When he finally took his mouth from hers, her breathing was ragged, and his own was laboured.

He said softly, 'Even when I thought the bid had failed, and you had been responsible, I was coming after you. You don't get rid of me that easily, Laura.'

Laura stared at him helplessly. 'I don't understand,' she whispered.

'It wasn't difficult to sort out,' he explained. 'Faced with two similar tenders, the company decided to opt for mine. They know me, they know the quality of my work, and it was fairly obvious that whoever submitted the other plans must have had access to mine at some stage.'

'But who? You said——'

He groaned, cupping her face in his hands, his thumb sliding over her cheek, moving down to nudge sensuously at the corner of her mouth. 'I know,' he said. 'I behaved like a fool. I'm sorry.' His eyes followed the action of his fingers, his gaze lingering on the full, ripe curve of her lips. Her lashes dusted her cheeks, and he moved closer, kissing her hungrily.

Laura savoured the moment, burying her fingers in the smooth material of his jacket, returning his kiss as if it might be the last. The last. . .

Reluctantly, she came to her senses, dragging her mouth from the tender passion of his embrace.

'But who—was it just coincidence, after all?' Confusion darkened her eyes.

'Oh, no,' he said flatly. 'It was all planned. There were only two people apart from myself who could have known anything of the final drawings—yourself and James.'

'But James wouldn't——'

'James did.'

Laura gasped, and he went on, 'He didn't do it intentionally. He'd had too much to drink, and his *friend* came along and obligingly listened to everything he had to say. It was perhaps unfortunate for James that Kevin's father happened to own a rival company to my own.'

Laura shuddered. Thinking aloud, she said, 'It must have been the night he took me to dinner. If I hadn't——' She stopped suddenly, and Daniel took her fingers in his own, rubbing them lightly.

'Don't start blaming yourself,' he said firmly. 'If there's any blame to be laid, it's on me, for jumping to conclusions, and for not pointing out to James that he ought to be on the lookout for sharks. It's a savage world out there. He's learned the hard way.'

Laura said hesitantly, 'Were you very angry with him?'

Daniel smiled faintly. 'I got over it. You caught me at a bad time, unfortunately, and got the brunt of my bad temper. It was only after you had gone that I thought over what I'd said, and I could have kicked myself. It didn't matter any more. Whatever you had done, whatever had gone wrong between us, we could sort it all out, if only I could talk to you, I was sure of that. But by then it was too late, you'd taken off into nowhere and I had the devil of a job on my hands to find you again.'

'How did you find me?' she asked.

'I had one or two leads that I was following up—taxi drivers, petrol stations, a list of accommodation to let that I was working my way through. It would have taken a long time, but I'd have got there in the end. Then I had a few choice words to say to James over the telephone, and he very quickly had second thoughts about heeding your warning to keep quiet about your new address. He wanted to make amends for the business of the leisure complex, and I asked him to write to you, dangling the carrot of a commission. I thought if we met on neutral ground there might be at least some chance of making headway.'

She looked at him from under her lashes. 'You are so devious,' she said softly. 'Don't you have a conscience?'

'Not if it means losing you again,' he answered bluntly, his dark eyes glinting. 'I've made too many mistakes already.' He drew her against the solid warmth of his body, his gaze moving over her possessively. 'Can't we start over, Laura? Begin again? I've made such a mess of things—can you forgive me? I can't bear to think that you will walk out of my life again. How can I persuade you that I can make you happy if you come back to me?'

Laura shook her head in bewilderment, and Daniel sucked in his breath audibly.

'I love you,' he said huskily. 'Doesn't that count for anything? I know I've a quick temper, I'm like a bear with a sore head sometimes, and I don't have as much privacy as I would like, but I love you, Laura. I want you to be my wife, I want you with me for always.'

He looked anguished, his face carved into tight, stricken lines, and Laura lifted a trembling hand to his face, stroking her fingers gently over the lean contours. 'You never said that before,' she whispered, and he frowned. 'About loving me,' she said.

He kissed the tips of her fingers, still held firmly in the palm of his hand. 'That cuts both ways,' he muttered. 'Have I been wrong in thinking you might care?'

Laura shook her head, trailing her fingers lightly over his mouth. 'I love you,' she whispered, 'but it hurts, Daniel. I'm so afraid it will be snatched away, that it isn't real.'

He moved slowly, but purposefully, pressing her into the cushions of the chesterfield, and proceeded to kiss her soundly for the next few minutes, all but taking her breath away. When she finally surfaced, he said thickly, 'Was that real enough for you? Or shall I demonstrate some more?'

She gave a tremulous sigh, and he nuzzled his mouth against her throat, letting his lips slide warmly across her smooth skin, and down over the silk of her blouse. 'I knew from the first that you were the woman for me,' he mumbled against the softness of her curves, 'but too many things got in the way. That isn't going to happen again. Will you marry me, Laura? We can live at Oakleigh, or we'll find somewhere else if you'd prefer——'

'It doesn't matter where we live,' she murmured, ousting the worried frown from his mouth with a kiss. 'As long as we're together. Didn't I tell you that I love you? How many times do you want me to prove it?'

He moved her gently back into the cushions and stared at her mouth in fascination. His finger traced the soft, full outline with infinite tenderness. 'I want to prove my love for you,' he said. 'Over and over, starting now.'

His hands caressed her slowly, curving over the

soft swell of her breasts, trembling a little, and that brought a sigh of contentment to her lips. He had always been able to incite her to a reckless passion, but knowing that she had the same effect on him sent a wild fever coursing through her body.

'I need you, Daniel,' she breathed raggedly. 'Without you I'm so miserable. Don't ever go away—I couldn't bear to lose you.'

He smiled down at her, hugging her into the warm circle of his arms. 'It seems I've waited a lifetime to hear you say that. You're stuck with me, sweetheart, from now to eternity.' He kissed her again, his hands moulding her to him with warm urgency, until all the longing and heated tension that was pent up inside threatened to spill over and send them both tumbling over the edge into a ceaseless whirlpool of desire.

Unsteadily, he dealt with her garments, shucking out of his own in turn. Her breath caught as she gazed on the rugged perfection of his body, then he came down to her, and her mind hazed over as his mouth played havoc with her senses, smoothing down over her rounded curves, across the flat plane of her stomach, seeking every tender, sensitive part of her. Her hands made an answering search over the hard-packed muscles of his arms and chest, along his spine, sliding tremulously in delicious exploration of his supple, magnificent strength.

Daniel groaned, shuddering against her. 'I can't wait, Laura. I want you so much, please don't make me wait.' He moved over her, his hands stroking the silken line of her thighs, provoking, enticing, until he had discovered her moist, inner warmth. He caressed he with a sensual expertise that tormented and delighted, until she pleaded for release, soft, choked cries tumbling from her lips. He entered her then, their bodies meshing, submerging, one with the other, scaling the heights together until the tumult of sensation reached its nerve-shattering peak, exploded, and they drifted, dazed, on a lazy, honeyed tide of drowsy passion.

Daniel surfaced slowly, and buried his face in the soft hollow of her throat. 'I love you,' he muttered thickly. 'We'll have to be married soon.'

She nodded, smiling, and mumbled against the sheen of his hair, 'But not right away, hmm?'

His head lifted sharply. 'You can't mean that,' he said, his voice roughened. 'I was thinking, only as long as it took to arrange a church.'

Her fingers moved lightly over the muscled perfection of his shoulders.

He groaned again, a deep, harsh sound in the back of his throat. 'Do you have any idea what your touch does to me?'

'Mmmm,' she said, her lips feathering over his smooth, supple skin. 'When do you have to be back in London to sign those papers?'

'Next week.'

'That should give us plenty of time to plan a wedding,' she murmured huskily, and Daniel's mouth curved in slow appreciation. Then he kissed her, long, and hard, and very, very thoroughly.

Three women, three loves . . .
Haunted by one dark,
forbidden secret.

ALIX ATKINSON

Boundaries

Margaret – a corner of he
heart would always remai
Karl's, but now she had t
reveal the secrets of the
passion which still had th
power to haunt and disturb

Miriam – the child of tha
forbidden love, hurt by he
mother's little love for he
had been seduced b
Israel's magic and the lov
of a special man.

Hannah – blonde an
delicate, was the child of
that love and in her blu
eyes, Margaret could agai
see Karl.

It was for the girl's sak
that the truth had to be tol
for only by confessing th
secrets of the past coul
Margaret give Hannah hop
for the future.

WORLDWIDE

NEW AUTHOR
SELECTION SURVEY 1991

Spare a few minutes to tell us your views about our
NEW AUTHOR SELECTION for 1991,
and we will send you a

<u>FREE Mills & Boon Romance</u>

as our thank you.

Dont forget to fill in your name and address, so that
we know where to send your FREE book!

Please tick the appropriate box to indicate your answers ✓

1 **How did you obtain your NEW AUTHOR SELECTION?**

Mills & Boon Reader Service ☐

W.H. Smith, John Menzies, another newsagent ☐

Boots, Woolworth, Department Store ☐

Supermarket ☐

Received as a gift ☐

Other (Please specify) _____

2 **If you bought the pack for yourself, what made you choose it?**

_____

_____

3 **If the pack was a gift, who bought it for you?**

_____

4 **a) Which of the four authors did you enjoy the most?**

_____

b) Why? _____

_____

5 Do you intend to read more Romances by the author that you enjoyed the most?

Yes ☐   No ☐   Not sure ☐

6 a) Which of the four authors did you enjoy the least?

_____

b) Why?_____

_____

7

Would you like to make any other comments about the New Author Selection?

_____

_____

_____

8 How many Mills & Boon Romances do you normally read?

Less than one a month ☐   Five to ten a month ☐

One a month ☐   More than ten a month ☐

Two to four a month ☐   Other (please specify)

_____

9 What is your age group?

16 – 24 ☐   35 – 44 ☐   55 – 64 ☐

25 – 34 ☐   45 – 54 ☐   65 plus ☐

Thank you for your help ——— **NO STAMP NEEDED** ——— NAP91A

Please send to: Mills & Boon Reader Service,
                   FREEPOST, P.O. Box 236, Croydon, CR9 9EL.

Mrs. / Ms. / Miss. / Mr. _____

Address _____

_____

_____

_____

_____ Postcode _____

mps MAILING PREFERENCE SERVICE